FIGHTING FOR US

Love Is Worth Fighting For Series Book 1

BELLA EMY

Victoria,

Thank you for your continued Support!

Bella ♡

Cover Designer: Just Write Creations
Editor: Angie Wade of Novel Nurse Editing
Proofreader: Janna Bethel

✿ Created with Vellum

Synopsis

LORENZO

I had it all.
A wonderful family with a loving wife who was my world and a beautiful baby girl.
I didn't need anything more to be rich in my eyes.
Then one day, everything changed and my world was ripped apart.
My wife, my everything, was taken from me, and I was left alone to raise our baby girl.
I was forced from late night sessions at the gym to changing diapers all by myself.
Thank God for the help I received from my parents and siblings or I would have been lost.
I accepted my fate of being alone with my baby girl and living life with just us two...
Until the day I met her, and she became everything worth fighting for.

CARISSA

Life was so perfect.
A loving fiancé, wonderful friends and family, and a job I adored.
Until one day, my world was turned upside down and the man I loved threw the promise of forever down the drain and walked out of my life.
The day he walked out of my door, I knew that everything I had ever grown up to believe in was a lie.

Love is unconditional but love sure as hell doesn't last forever.

The vow to love me for the rest of our lives ended quickly as he pulled away from me, and buried himself in the arms of his ex.

I was left alone, cursing the male species and everyone who had found their happily ever after.

My sister and my best friend were the only ones there for me...

Until the day I met him, and he became everything worth fighting for.

To my family and friends for always supporting me and being there for me when I need you most.

❤

Contents

Introduction

Fighting for Us is the first book of the
Love is Worth Fighting For Series.

For more information on the series, please visit
www.BellaEmy.com

To stay up to date with all the series information, please
make sure you are subscribed to my newsletter at:
bit.ly/BellaEmySubscribe

Chapter One

LORENZO

I sit at my wife's side in a plastic chair, holding on to her hand. We've been like this for hours, but there's been no response from her whatsoever. I let out a deep sigh; there is nothing else I can do with this hand of cards we've been dealt. This is our life now, and as much as I wish things were different, I know no amount of wishing or praying can save us.

I rub my thumb over her small hand again and again, hoping to get any kind of response. But there's nothing. Not a twitch, not a jerk. Her tiny hand rests motionless in my large one.

Sylvia is a petite woman, and I have always towered over her. With me being an ex-Navy SEAL, she used to call me her lion. She always used to say I could protect her from anything.

And of course, I could have.

Except this.

I hang my head low as the depressing realization of something completely out of my control takes over. I hate myself for not being able to save her. I hate myself for letting her down. As her partner, I should be able to help her, to make her feel happy and safe once more, but she's so far gone, nothing I do will bring her back to me the way she used to be.

I can't protect her.

I can't save her.

I can't heal her pain.

I'm worthless to her. What good is being her husband, a retired man in uniform, if I can't protect the one I love? It doesn't make any sense. Me sitting here beside her, not able to do a damn thing to help this fucking situation, is pissing me off.

The nurses come in every so often to check her vitals, but there is no change in her condition. I hang my head down once they're gone, and I pray in silence.

Yeah, prayers… like they have done me any good. It's been months, yet nothing has changed.

Sylvia has been hanging on by a thread, fighting for her life. And of course, everything hit us at once: we got married three years ago after dating for five years, had a baby girl just four months ago, and now, for the past two months, she's been in this damn hospital room fighting every single day for her life. She hasn't even been able to enjoy motherhood. Lord knows she wanted a baby for as long as I can remember. And then, after just six months of trying, BAM! Two pink lines on a pregnancy test confirmed we were expecting our first bundle of joy. Little did we know Gianna would be our only child together.

Sylvia was the happiest preggo around. Her pregnancy went well, although it wasn't a piece of cake. With complicated medical history on her side, we had a few scares, but bed rest and multiple doctor visits had helped get her through.

Anyway, fast forward to August sixteenth of this past year, and out came little Gianna Michelle Trevano. She was a healthy six-pound–five-ounce baby girl with her mother's piercing blue eyes and cute button nose and my smile. I'd seen Sylvia in the happiest of times, but none of those moments compared to the radiating smile on her face the moment they placed Gianna into her arms. The picture we had taken of her at that moment is the wallpaper on my phone.

When October rolled along, Sylvia started complaining of headaches. She'd lie down for a few hours while I took care of Gianna. Well, sooner rather than later, hours turned to days and days turned to weeks, and that was when I brought her in to see a doctor. Her headaches were getting longer and occurring more frequently. Something was up; I just knew it.

I had no idea it would be this.

And now, in the middle of December, my beautiful Sylvia is barely hanging on. I don't know how much more of this I can take. She used to wake up for minutes at a time, but when she did, she would scream and cry out in pain. She's lost a vast amount of weight in such a short amount of time. Her once full golden locks are now limp strands of a washed out, faded yellow. Her voice hoarse, her cheeks barren… She's dying, and I'm dying alongside her.

What kind of life is this without her? She was supposed to be my forever, my one true love, and now? Now she's being ripped away from me, and I can't take it.

To see her suffering like this breaks my heart. And to think, I have a baby girl at home who needs her. Gia needs her mother. I can't raise my daughter on my own. I'm scared, and I don't know how I'm going to do it. I'm thankful for my parents and siblings who are with Gianna while I've been here alone, wondering again if today is the day I have to say good-bye to my wife forever.

I snap my head up and look at the ceiling. As I shake my head, the rage inside me feels as though it wants to rip through these damn four walls. I'm tired of being here, tired of having to stay in this room, waiting for the worst. I want to take Sylvia home so we can be with our baby girl, so we can be a family again. I want her to be better, and I want our life back.

But it's not coming back. Not after what the doctors are telling us. She's hanging on by a thread, and it's only a matter of time before she's taken from me. We're never going back to the way things should be, and she's never coming back to me. She's never going to open her eyes and look at me with her warm, caring smile ever again.

A tear falls from my eye as realization kicks in. I'm not ready to let her go. I don't want to.

I'm twenty-eight years old. How can it be possible that I'm about to lose her? We had our whole lives planned. We were supposed to grow old together. This… This fucking nightmare was never in the plans we had set out for one another.

More tears cascade down my cheeks. This is a damn horror movie, not my life. I hang my head and grab it on both sides.

"You hanging in there, sugar?"

I snap my head up, wiping my cheek, at the sound of one of the night nurses coming into the room. Cynthia, a sixty-five-year-old widow and mother of three, is our regular nurse on Tuesdays, Thursdays, Saturdays, and Sundays. Originally from the South, she moved up to New Jersey when her husband passed a few years ago.

"Hi, Cynthia," I respond, running a hand through my thick, dark hair. "How's she doing?"

Cynthia checks my wife's pulse, then takes her temperature. She frowns. "No change. You getting any sleep?"

"Sure." I lie, and she knows it.

She throws me a look confirming she's aware I'm fibbing, and I shrug. "How can I sleep?"

Cynthia nods. "Listen, baby. I know what you're going through better than anyone else, but you need to take care of

4

yourself and be there for little Gia. We're here for Sylvia... You know she's in good hands."

I nod in return. "I know... It's just difficult."

She writes something on Sylvia's chart and turns to face me once more. "Oh, I know it is, sugar. But you can't let this beat you down. Sylvia needs you to keep your promise."

"Promise?" I question with furrowed brows.

Cynthia folds her arms across her chest. "Well, of course, baby. The moment she got pregnant with your daughter, you both made a promise to one another that you'd be there and step up should something happen to one of you. It's your turn to step up and make sure you're putting your baby girl first."

"I'm trying, but I don't want to leave my wife's side... especially not now."

"I know that, sugar. I'm not saying to leave right now. I know how crucial her condition is at this moment. But when you can sneak in some shut eye, you've got to try to. And that's the first step of how you can be there for Gianna." She throws me another knowing look.

I nod once more. She walks up to Sylvia, places a hand on her forehead, and tells me she'll be back in a few hours.

Once she's gone, I pull out my cell phone from my pocket. It's just after eleven. I decide to text my brother, Massimo, or Max as we call him, to see how things are going at my house.

Me: How's it going? Gianna asleep?

Max: She just went down not too long ago... had woken up cuz she was wet. I'm glad Marianna is here with me cuz I still can't change a diaper for the life of me LOL.

I chuckle to myself, reading my brother's response.

Me: LOL. One day you'll have your own kids.
One day you'll learn.

Max: Yeah, not for now! Gigi's more than enough!
How's Sylvs?

I frown at the mention of the nickname he'd given my wife the moment I told him about her.

Me: No change.

I can't bear to add anything further. I can't bear to tell him I'm on the verge of a fucking breakdown.

Max: Shit.

I'm about to compose a reply when a blaring sound from the ventilator my wife is hooked up to goes off. Something's not right. My eyes meet the machine, and there, right before my eyes, a green horizontal line confirms my worst nightmare.

I jump to my feet, screaming my wife's name.

It's as if what happens next is a scene from a movie.

Everything slows.

Nurses and doctors rush in to be at Sylvia's side.

"Sugar, come with me," Cynthia demands, placing an arm over my shoulder. She wills me out of the room with my head swimming between fighting against her and wanting to them to help. "Come on, baby… You can't stay here…"

Tears fall from the corners of my eyes yet again as fear grips the back of my throat. "N-no, I… I…"

Doctors crowd around Sylvia and place resuscitators on her chest, then try desperately to bring her back.

They try and fail miserably each time.

Oh my God, this can't be it.

This can't be the day I lose my wife.

"No! I have to stay with my wife.... Sylvia, oh God, sweetheart!" Tears continue streaming down my face.

Cynthia pulls me into an embrace, and I let everything out onto her shoulder. "Shhh, I know, baby... I know," she says, rubbing my back.

I can't stop the tears, but when I finally do, it's hours later, and my Sylvia, my darling wife, is gone.

Chapter Two

LORENZO

Five years later…

I toss my bag over my shoulder, and right as I'm about to exit the locker room, Ryker throws a white piece of cloth at me. I grab it just in time to realize it's his sweaty undershirt. Dude is nasty, but he's my best friend. Still, I scowl and drop it to the floor, throwing him a glare. He's chuckling.

"Just testing your reflexes, man," he says, slamming his locker shut.

"Yeah, yeah. Keep that shit up and you'll be testing something else," I warn.

He leans against his locker, folding his arms. "Oh, yeah? And what's that supposed to mean?"

I walk over to him and shove two fingers against his chest. "That if you don't watch it…" I point toward the doors leading to the main area of the gym. "You'll find yourself in that ring with me. And it won't be for practice." Just beyond those very doors is the octagon ring where we practice for events.

Ryker has never faced me in any event, but we practice together all the time. I'm glad because how are you supposed to fight your best friend? I'd kill him. I can't help it that my record is almost flawless. Every match I've been in, besides the first one from when I started, I've been undefeated. But hey, it's all right. I'm planning on getting my revenge on Dennis "The Big Shot" Mavis at the next chance I get. I'll have my turn. I'll get my belt and the cash that goes with it too.

Hell, I deserve something for everything I've been through. At least I found a good way to channel my inner anger. I could've turned out to be an alcoholic deadbeat dad. But I'm not.

"Lorenzo Trevano, it would be an honor to rumble with you inside the cage," Ryker says, finally picking up his undershirt.

Ryker and I will both be fighting in the upcoming event. It's the biggest one of the year, and although we are not fighting against each other, the two of us will be giving it our all to win.

I chuckle and head toward the door. "Don't forget to shut off the lights and lock up on your way out. I'll catch you later, Ryke."

"Later," he responds.

I walk out of the building, and the chill in the air hits my cheeks. It feels good. The cold, late-November wind blows, whooshing through the area. After working up a sweat during practice, the cool breeze is a nice welcome.

I unlock the doors of my black four-seater pickup truck and throw my bag in the back as I hop in behind the wheel. With my buckle clasped and my mirrors checked, I start on my way home.

It's after eleven at night, but this is my norm. We're getting ready for the next UFC meet, which is in a few days, and I'm psyched. I'm so ready to get inside that cage and go head-to-head with my opponents. There's nothing like the rush I get when that bell rings and it's go time. Nothing.

Well, maybe there is something, but that's a story I refuse to get into right now. Or ever. That part of my life died with—

I let out a deep breath, shake my head, and think about my baby girl. Thoughts of her always put a smile on my face, no matter what type of day I'm having. It was hard in the beginning, to pick up the pieces and trudge on, but now, I can't picture my life without her. She's my sunshine and the light of my life. I'm a total baby-girl's daddy.

I'm sure Gianna is already out by now... at least I hope so, for poor Max's sake. She's a feisty little one with big blue eyes and chunky rosy cheeks, and she can talk at a hundred miles per second. She's the cutest little thing under three feet I ever did see. Sure, I'm biased, but what good dad isn't? She's my princess.

I chuckle, thinking back to the last conversation we had. She started by asking me if kittens and puppies could understand us when we talk to them and ended by asking me if sharks have cousins.

As I pull up to my driveway, I see my brother's Bronco exactly where he parked it before I left, just two houses up.

I kill the engine, hop out of my truck, and grab my bag from the back seat. Slinging it over my shoulder, I shut the door, lock the car, and march up the walkway.

When I step foot inside my home, I see Max looking like a drunk, passed out on the couch with his mouth open. I contemplate for a second about throwing something into it but decide against it, chuckling to myself. Looks like little Gia wore him out. I'll let him sleep for another few minutes while I put my stuff away and check on my baby girl.

I place my bag inside the hallway closet and make my way toward Gia's bedroom. Her door is slightly cracked, so I open it a tad bit more and peek in. I smile as I watch my princess in a deep slumber. She looks so peaceful.

I tiptoe in and cautiously walk toward her. The rise and

fall of her chest confirms she must already be on her fifth dream or so of the night. I bend down to push her dark-brown hair out of her face and place a kiss on her forehead. Thankfully, she doesn't even stir.

"Sweet dreams, princess," I whisper.

I leave her room, satisfied, and walk back out into the living room. My brother is still passed out.

I laugh to myself and say, "Gianna wear you out again?"

Max jumps up. "Huh? What?" He turns his head from left to right. "Oh, you're back. What time is it?"

I smile, still amused. "Just after eleven thirty."

He stretches, yawning. "Damn, one minute we're watching *Cinderella*, and the next minute, the two of us are knocked out in dreamland. I woke up during the credits and placed her in her bed."

The TV is still on, and another Disney classic movie is playing.

I nod. "Yeah, I just checked on her. She's fast asleep. Thanks, man."

He takes a step forward. "Don't mention it, Enz. I love that little munchkin."

I smile again. "I know you do. But it can't be easy coming here right after your day job to hang out with a five-year-old so her dad can go do his thing."

He slaps a hand on my back. "That's what family is for, bro. I wouldn't have it any other way."

He's right. As a family, we've always been tightly knit. My two siblings, he and his twin, Marianna, and I have always been close. Our parents raised us to understand that family always comes first, and as long as we've got each other, everything else will always work itself out.

That's what I believe in anyway, but ever since that dreadful day five years ago when I lost her, I haven't known what to do. Part of my family is gone… How can things ever work themselves out?

Not wanting to let my brother see me dwell on my past, I ask about our sister. "Marianna doing okay?"

"Yeah, you know she called in to check on us around six. I think she wants to stop by tomorrow. Her job's kicking her ass right now."

My sister is a pediatrician at her office downtown. She loves working with children, but since it's cold and flu season, she's seeing many sick kids. Maybe it's the reason she's been looking so beat up, but honestly, I think it's her husband, Jordan. The bastard...

"That's fine. I know she's busy."

Max nods and stretches once more. "Yeah, but you know she can't stay away from the little one too long."

I smile. What he says is true. My siblings and parents have always been obsessed with my little girl. She's their first niece and granddaughter, so of course she's special to them. I'm fortunate that they've always been here for me and Gianna.

"I'd better run. The blaring alarm isn't going to have mercy on me at five a.m. Office life sucks sometimes." Max walks to the front door, and I follow closely behind him.

"I know, man."

Unlike Max, I don't have to be up until seven. I'll get ready and take Gianna to school. While she's there, I run errands and keep up the house until it's time to pick her up again. Then, before I head to work, Max comes to stay with her. MMA is my job. Well, it's my company. I own the gym: Lorenzo's Fitness Center. It's not your typical nine-to-five, but along with competing and winning, owning the place brings in cash. Thanks to my pension from my navy days, I was able to open my own gym and afford to do what I love. I mean, I can't think of anything else I would rather be doing than taking out my anger and frustration in the ring. Lord knows I have a ton of it, plus some to spare.

"Have a good night, Enz. Get some sleep." Max steps out the front door.

"Night, man. Drive safe." I lock the door behind him and turn off the television.

I head to the bathroom and jump in the shower. I lather and rinse in record time; I'm so ready to hit the sack and, hopefully, pass out within minutes.

Once I finish toweling off, I put on a pair of gray boxer briefs and climb into bed. I never sleep with a shirt on. Hell, I used to sleep naked back in the day. If I lived alone, I probably still would.

I turn on the television and flip through channels, not really caring for much of anything I'm seeing.

Then, as I come across channel 136, I see it. *Just Married*, the 2003 romantic comedy with Ashton Kutcher and Brittany Murphy. Unbridled tears form in my eyes as memories come storming into my mind. This was Sylvia's favorite movie, and we had seen it together so many times. Now I'm watching it alone.

It's been five years since she's been gone, and I still can't help but cry when things like this happen. Something as silly as a movie we used to watch together sends me on a spiral of memories, leading to me falling into a bottomless pit of despair.

My Sylvia. My everything. She's gone, and I miss her so goddamn much. I miss our family as it used to be. I miss having someone I can talk to about my day or listen to about theirs. I miss having her here with me, sharing this life we were meant to have together. I miss hearing her sweet voice in the morning or the sound of it as she'd sing in the shower. I miss her cooking and all the home-cooked meals she'd make me. I miss her beautiful smile that would light up a room. I miss the sound of her laughter and the way she'd lie her head on my chest as we'd cuddle in bed together. I miss her scent and the looks she would give me filled with lust and desire, confirming she wanted only me. I miss taking her body in the middle of the night and sending her into an oblivion each time we'd make love.

I miss everything about her. Most of all, I just miss her. I miss having her here with me, especially now as our little girl is growing up. It sucks, and it's not fair. And I know it probably makes me look soft, being a UFC fighter who is so dedicated to his love, but I can't help it. She was my everything. I miss her like crazy. We were supposed to share this life together. We were supposed to raise kids and grandkids, growing old together. Now the promise of forever is just forever gone.

Somewhere between the couple arriving in Italy and experiencing their first fight as newlyweds, I doze off, succumbing to much-needed sleep.

Chapter Three

CARISSA

"Hot! That's all I can say, freaking hot as fire!"

"Don't bother. She's not interested."

I peek a glance over the book I'm reading at my best friend, Emerson, or Emy, who's trying to convince me to head out basically every night. My sister, Shannon, tells her not to waste her time.

"Oooh, I got a look!" Emy says to Shannon.

I can't help but smirk.

Shannon rolls her eyes. "It doesn't matter. The girl is hopeless. You'd think she'd want to get laid again some day."

I gasp, put my book down, and toss a throw pillow at Shannon from my seat on the couch. I miss, and the two of them crack up.

"Yeah, especially since she's always around those hot male nurses and doctors... Carissa, how do you contain yourself?" Emy asks.

"Keep it up, bitches," I say, picking my book back up. I work at the hospital downtown.

Emy drops to her knees and crawls toward me with a flyer in one of her hands.

My eyes dart in her direction, and she's sporting the

saddest frown I've ever seen. I want to burst with laughter because this is ridiculous.

Seriously, is this all that matters to the two of them? Going out and meeting guys? Partying and drinking until they pass out God knows where? I'm not into it. I never have been, and honestly, I never want to hear about the male species ever again, and they both know it. It's not like it's something new. It's been like this for the past three years. I don't know why it's so hard for them to understand. It's like they can't live without dick.

Well, I can. I know I can.

"You need to jump off your feelings of being all anti-dick and start jumping into a man's bed… preferably one with a nice, big cock." Emy flips her hair back.

Shannon laughs. "Miss No Filter." Her dazzling three-karat engagement ring sparkles in the light. She's engaged to her fiancé, Christopher, and they've been together for two years.

Emy throws her a proud grin. "That's right. I am Miss No Filter, and I don't give a fuck. I tell you how it is for your own good, sweetie. And you, my love, definitely need some D in your life. And by D, I mean dick."

"I know what you mean!" I throw my hands up in exasperation. There's no winning with these two. I totally give up.

"Carissa! Please!" Emy shouts as she grabs onto my arms and pulls back and forth. "I mean, look at the size of those biceps! Look at that smirk… ugh, he's fucking gorgeous! Tell me this poster alone doesn't make your panties wet!"

Shannon is guffawing. "Oh my God! Girl! I can't with you!"

"Jesus, Emy! Chill!" I yell, rising from the couch.

Emy joins Shannon in a fit of giggles. I'm going to kill these two.

"How can you two be so damn—"

"Turned on?" Emy interrupts, cutting me off.

"Horny… definitely horny after looking at that and imagining the things—"

My eyes widen, and I cross my arms across my chest. "Shannon, you too? Your man would not approve."

Shannon comes to my side and drapes an arm across my shoulders. "It's a harmless comment. I'm not cheating on Chris. I love him. But come on, li'l sis. You have to admit that whoever he is, he is one fine piece of man meat… I can't blame Emy for trying to get us to go with her. Well, you. I'm definitely going with."

"Thank you, Shannon!" Emy exclaims, rising to her feet. She takes a few steps to reach us and holds out the flyer for us to see.

Honestly, I hadn't even glanced at it when she first waved it around. It's an advertisement for some big MMA fight coming up next month. Now, I'm looking at what they're going crazy over. Some guy with his arms crossed—huge arms, might I add—is standing against a ring wearing a devilish smirk. A bunch of other muscle heads are to his left and right. Sure, he's not bad looking, but like I said before, I'm not interested.

"Look, Em… She's not saying anything. I think Guns got her attention… fin-a-fucking-ly!" Shannon states.

"I know, for real," Emy says.

I furrow my brows and look at my sister. "Guns? I don't see any weapons on this flyer." I know what she's talking about, but I love pulling their chain.

Once again, the two of them are cracking up.

Once Shannon catches her breath, she says, "Oh, Carissa. Sometimes I wonder if you were adopted. *Guns...* as in massive arms… not pistols."

"Well, I wouldn't mind seeing his pistol…" Emy says.

"Me neither!" Shannon chuckles.

I give the flyer another glance and then roll my eyes. "You

two are ridiculous. I swear." I walk back to the couch and take a seat.

Shannon sits on the love seat across from me, pulling her cell phone from her pocket. "I give up."

Emy, instead, takes a seat right next to me. "Carissa, my best friend whom I've known since we were in kindergarten, please don't make me drag you out of this house on the fifth to witness the eye candy the good Lord has blessed us with."

Once again, I roll my eyes. "Emy, take Shannon's advice and give up. I'm not attending any stupid AMM event."

"MMA!" she shouts. "You know, UFC?"

I chuckle. "I know. I'm just trying to get under your skin like you're getting under mine."

I pick up my book, *Anna Karenina*, and dive back into the scene where Anna first meets Count Vronsky at the train station. No matter how many times I read this book, it always gets to me. Shannon and Emy are always calling me a bookworm, but I don't care. I'm a sucker for romance novels —particularly this Tolstoy one.

I wonder if it's because I've always wished for a love like the ones I read in books. Okay, not particularly a love like the one I'm currently reading about, but the passion for sure. Maybe it's because this is fiction, and I know it doesn't really happen in life. I'll say that's the reason so I don't feel so bad about my own shortcomings in the romance department.

Sure, I've had a couple of boyfriends throughout my thirty-two years, but none of them have ever gotten me anywhere. My last was a complete disaster.

Well, he wasn't my boyfriend when we split up. He was my fiancé, and he completely destroyed me after being with him for two and a half years.

What a complete fucking waste.

"Carissa," Emy whispers to grab my attention once more. This time, I'm not totally mad at her. I'm thankful she's pulled me out of my thoughts because every time I think of Steve, I want to strangle someone.

Placing my book to the side, I turn to face Emy.

"Shit, girl. I know that look. Are you thinking of that dickhead again?"

She knows me too well. All I do is shrug.

"I swear I'm going to kill that son of a bitch! Look at what he's done to my sister! It's been three years, and she's still hurting from what that asshole did to her!"

"I'm fine!" I snap, facing Shannon.

"Carissa, listen to me," Emy says. "Okay, forget this UFC event coming up in two weeks. We'll discuss that another time. Let's go out tonight and have a few drinks. It'll be fun. We haven't done that in so long."

"What's the point? I hate drinking," I respond.

"To get our mind off shit. Come on, li'l sis. We'll have a good time and make jokes," Shannon says.

She's got a point. Maybe going out with them will allow me to forget my troubles and Mr. Douchebag for a while. It can't hurt to have a little fun. Still, I want to mess with them just a bit longer. "I don't know. I'm at this really great part in my book—"

"Carissa!" the two of them shout in unison.

I laugh. "Okay, okay. I'll go."

"Yes!" Emy jumps up from the couch. "Bottoms Up, here we come!

I quickly interrupt her celebratory dance. "But… no funny business. Meaning it'll just be us girls, without you two trying to set me up with any morons." I point at the two of them.

Shannon rises from her seat. "Deal. I'm going home to change. I'll pick you both up in about two hours. Be ready."

"Oh, we will!" Emy says in a singsong voice as Shannon heads out the door.

"I hope I haven't made a grave mistake." I frown. Maybe I gave in a bit too soon.

Emy laughs. "It's going to be fine. And then, when you see how much fun tonight is going to be, you're going to beg us to go out again tomorrow night."

"Tomorrow night? I don't think so. Two nights in a row is asking a bit much."

Emy nods her head. "I don't care about tomorrow. I'm just saying it's going to be great."

"I hope you're right."

"I always am," Emy says with a smug grin.

Somehow, I'm not totally convinced, but what the hell. It's only a couple of drinks with my friend and sister. What could be so bad?

Chapter Four

LORENZO

Every other weekend, I get together with my brother and sister, and we grab either a bite to eat or some drinks.

Tonight, on this miserable Friday as a nasty rainstorm blows through our area, I find myself with Max and Marianna at the bar, Bottoms Up. My mother and father pick up Gianna every other weekend to spoil her like no tomorrow. I wasn't thrilled about the arrangement at first because she is my responsibility, and when I don't have her with me, it sometimes feels as though I'm not doing what I'm supposed to be doing. But over time, I've grown accustomed to it. They think I need to recuperate and recharge. Yes, having a five-year-old daughter is a lot of work and is exhausting at times, especially when my job is so physical, but I love my little girl. I love spending time with her, and usually on weekends, we do something fun outside of our home.

I know my parents mean well. Plus, they love having her over and bonding with her so I can find some type of normalcy—or rather, what they believe is normalcy for a single guy my age.

They say single. I still say widowed. I'm not single. I still love my wife, even if she's no longer with me here on Earth. She'll always be in my heart.

Anyway, they would love for me to meet someone on one of my off weekends from being with my daughter. I know they hate that we're alone, but I'm not looking to pick up women or find a replacement for Sylvia. There is no one who will ever replace my love. You'd think by now they'd understand.

So, to make them happy, I spend time with the two people I can count on no matter what: my brother and sister.

I'm the oldest, followed by Max and then Marianna. Well, it's funny because they're only a minute apart. Yeah, they're twins, but they couldn't be more different if they tried.

Max and I look a lot alike. We both take after our mother, while Marianna is the spitting image of our father, except for her long hair, pretty face, and boobs.

"I still don't think it's a good idea," Marianna says, bringing me out of my musings.

Max intervenes. "Why? I think it's fine. It's been five years."

I sip on my beer and watch Marianna throw him the glare I knew was coming. These two usually go at it when they differ in opinion... which is most of the time.

"Why? *Why?* Because! That's precisely the reason! Five years!"

Max shakes his head. "It's not the first big match since she's been gone, Mari."

Marianna rolls her eyes, annoyance obviously on her face. "It doesn't matter. It's the fifth anniversary. He should never take part in any match on December fifth," she responds as if I'm not sitting right here in between the two of them. It's a small circular table, so we're all facing one another.

I close my eyes and take another sip. Thinking I'd best say something, I take a deep breath and slowly open my eyes to look directly at Marianna. "Mari, it's fine. I'll be okay, and I definitely have to take part in this match. I've been training for it for months. I'll be okay."

Marianna shakes her head. "I don't think it's smart for you to take part in the match. I know you have built up anger because of... well, everything."

"He's fine, Marianna. You heard it straight from the horse's mouth," Max says.

Marianna turns to face Max. "I'm worried about him, Max. You don't understand because you're a guy."

He chuckles. "What's that supposed to mean?"

"I'm worried he's going to get hurt... or worse, hurt someone else, maybe more."

They throw glances at me, and I almost spit out my beer. Yes, I've been known to have a temper. I've had built-up anger since Sylvia's passing, but isn't that natural? I lost someone who meant the world to me. It wasn't fair. I've been depressed, and lost, and downright angry. It's the main reason why I turned to MMA fighting. I thought it would be a positive way to channel my feelings. I need to unleash my inner beast. Plus, my brother has a temper too. I think every guy in my family does.

"Guys, I'll be fine. And I won't hurt anyone... *that bad.*" I give them a smug grin.

Marianna rolls her eyes while Max laughs.

"Ugh! Lorenzo! I give up with you! I'm going to have Mom talk you out of it," Marianna says and takes a sip from her glass.

I'm about to tell her that not even Mom can convince me not to partake in the event on the fifth, but as I'm about to respond, my eyes dart toward the door.

The ringing of the bell above it caught my attention, but the woman walking in behind two other ladies is holding it. She pulls a red-and-white striped candy cane out of her mouth and keeps it in between matching crimson lips for a few seconds.

Luscious, plump crimson lips. *Damn.*

I shake my head and look away, but I glance back at her as she makes her way to a table.

Long brown hair cascading down her back and big brown eyes make me stare. Pink cheeks and a pretty smile that is now visible grace her face, lighting up the dimly lit bar. *Wow.*

She's got a small frame, but her curves are evident as she slips her wet coat off. She's wearing a white top and skin-tight denim jeans. Heeled boots sit on her feet.

I take a long swig of my beer. I need to think of something else.

"Really, please give it some more thought, Enz. I would hate to see something bad happen," Marianna says. I know she's been talking for a minute, but I've been distracted, and that's all I've really heard her say in the past couple of minutes.

I turn my glance away from Luscious Lips and face Marianna.

Shit, did I really just give this woman I don't even know a nickname? And that nickname?

Okay, it's been a long time since I've last been intimate with someone. Sylvia was the last person I've been with. I haven't had the urge to be intimate with anyone since. I don't now either, but somehow I gave a name to this stranger.

Luscious Lips? What the hell? Yeah, she does have some nice lips that I imagine she can do amazing things with, but…

Damn, it's not my fault. The way she's sucking on that candy cane is really distracting. Fuck.

I shake my head and decide to answer Marianna. She's still staring at me, waiting for me to say something. I pick Marianna's hand up from the table and place a kiss on it to reassure her. "I'll be careful, sis. I promise."

Marianna lets out an audible breath and smiles. I think I've gotten through to her. Finally.

"Okay, big bro. I trust you. But you know I'll still be right there, cheering you on and ready to kick your butt if things get out of hand." She chuckles.

"Mari, you're so tiny. You wouldn't be able to do a damn thing," Max says.

"And though she be but little, she is fierce," she says, quoting Helena from *A Midsummer Night's Dream*, still smiling as she rises from her seat. It's her favorite line from Shakespeare, and she says it often since she's tiny, standing at only five foot two inches.

She looks at her phone, scrolling through it. "Dammit, he still hasn't responded. Maybe the service is bad here… I'm going out back to see if it makes a difference. Don't you two get into any trouble while I'm gone." She throws us both a warning look, pointing at us, and then pushes in her chair.

"We'll try not to," Max says as she walks away.

"She still hasn't heard back from Jordan?" I ask.

Max shrugs. "I don't know. She hasn't talked too much about him. But I guess he hasn't called her back."

Of course not. Piece of shit. I swear one of these days I'm going to wring his fucking neck and hang him from his nuts.

Max drains the remnants of his beer. "Anyway, you wanna tell me what that's all about?" He motions up with his chin, but I don't know what he's talking about.

I furrow my brows. "What?"

"Over there… *Trouble.* You know, the pretty little thing you've been ogling since she walked in here. She looks like trouble."

"What the hell are you talking about? I haven't been ogling anyone," I say a bit defensively.

Max chuckles. "Yeah right, Enz. I'm not blind. I've seen her, and I've seen you staring. It's not a bad thing, bro."

"I still have no idea what you're talking about," I lie.

He's not buying it. "Uh-huh. Well, whatever. You wanna play that game, fine. But check her out. To the left, white top, fucking amazing lips, and pretty brown eyes. She's sitting in between two chicks who could pass for her sisters or cousins or something."

Yeah, he knows I've been checking her out, but I need to pretend like I haven't seen her until now. I look over at where he mentioned.

"Oh, her," I respond.

He chuckles. "*Oh, her?* You're hilarious."

I turn my glance back toward him and shrug like it's nothing. "Okay, she's nice looking. What's your point?" I take the final sip of my beer.

He shakes his head with a smirk. "*Nice looking.* My point is that you're a man, and every man has needs. It's been a long time since... well, you know. It's okay to see other women you're attracted to and possibly talk to them. It's not a crime, and it's not wrong."

I chuckle, but it's void of humor. My anger is starting to flare, and I don't like where his words are going. The last thing I want is to get into an argument with my brother. "You're crazy, Max."

"I'm not. You probably feel guilty about it, but Enz, it's fine, and you have no reason to feel like that. It would be a totally different thing if Sylvs were still here and you were having thoughts or feelings about another woman, but—"

"That's enough!" I say, slamming my fist onto the table, just in time for Marianna to walk back, horrified and witnessing my anger firsthand.

"What's going on here?" She pulls out her chair.

"Don't bother taking a seat. It's time to leave," I snarl.

"What? Dude, we just got here twenty minutes ago," Max says.

I glare at him. Smoke has got to be visibly coming out of my ears.

I take a breath and try to compose myself.

"Fine, you guys stay. I'm out of here." I rise from my seat

and walk away without saying another word. Good thing I met them here and had come in my own car.

"Lorenzo!" I hear Marianna call out to me, but I don't bother answering her or turning around.

As I walk toward the door, I glance over at the mystery woman who caused this whole commotion. It's her fault this shit started in the first place.

Our eyes lock for the first time.

I quickly pull my stare away and walk out the door. I need to go home and forget this night. What a disaster. Thanks a lot, Luscious Lips.

Chapter Five

CARISSA

"Wow. Someone is definitely not getting any tonight," Emy states and Shannon chuckles.

"What?" I ask, turning my gaze from the door to look at them.

I was watching a guy as he stormed out of the building. He was intimidating. I've never seen a guy up close that massive before. Plus, he didn't even look all that friendly. He looked downright scary. I wonder what had gotten him so upset.

The woman three tables over called out to him. Lorenzo, she called, but he didn't stop. I wonder if she's his wife. Something she did upset him because he didn't even acknowledge her.

When our eyes met, it was as if he were looking right into my soul. It sent goose bumps down my spine.

"I'm just saying, that lady must have really pissed that guy off for him to walk out of here the way he did, without even looking back at her," Emy says.

"Yeah, but he sure did give you a captivating stare," Shannon says, turning to face me.

"What are you talking about?" I ask.

The girls turn to face one another and smirk.

"Girl, please. Don't even lie and say you didn't notice because you totally stared back at him. And I can't even blame you. He was gorgeous," Emy states, then takes a sip from her cup.

Dammit, they noticed.

Shannon nods, looking at Emy. "He was really gorgeous."

"And I think his anger added to his hotness... Like, can you imagine the damage he would do to a girl being that full of rage? Just lying underneath him? Oh my God... I would love to find out," Emy says.

I roll my eyes. "You two are insane."

Shannon pushes her hair out of her eyes. "Carissa, I'm sorry, but Em is right... He looks like he could literally destroy somebody, and I would love to be on the receiving end as well, just saying." She holds up her hands defensively and says, "If I were single, of course."

I roll my eyes again.

Emy places a hand underneath her chin. "I'm really curious as to why I've never seen any of them before. This isn't that big of a town."

"Maybe they don't get out much," Shannon states.

"Then macho man who just left would be perfect for Carissa." Emy smiles at me, her dark hair glimmering in the low lighting above our heads.

Shaking my head, I bite off a piece of candy cane and look back at the table where the furious man was sitting. The two other people, a man and a woman, who were sitting with him are still there, but now they're bickering about something I can't make out. The man looks a lot like him. He could pass for his brother. The woman on the other hand looks nothing like either one. It's what makes me think she's his wife or girlfriend. But if so, something still doesn't add up.

"Cariss, are you ever going to pick up your drink and down it?" Shannon asks.

"Yeah, put the candy cane down and drink, woman!" Emy says.

I shrug. I'm not a big drinker. I don't like the feeling I get afterward. "Maybe."

Both of them roll their eyes. Surprise, surprise.

"One day we'll get her to throw them back... one day," Emy says.

"Yeah and then I bet she'll drink both of us under the table." Shannon laughs and takes another sip.

Rolling my eyes yet again, I say, "You two are something else. Do you know that?"

"We do," they say in unison. You'd think these two were best friends and I'm just the third wheel.

"Anyway, back to the match coming up in two weeks... You're going to come, right?" Emy asks, fluttering her eyelashes at me.

"What?"

Emy pulls out the same flyer from earlier and places it down onto the table. "Two weeks. Straight fire. Look at these hotties."

I stare at the ad in front of me but don't really know what to say. Both of them want me to go, but I'm not sure I want to.

Shannon bites down on her bottom lip. "They are all freaking hot, but Guns is definitely the hottest one," she says, pointing at the man in the center, the one she had nicknamed earlier today at my apartment.

Emy lets out a sigh. "He really is. What I would give to see him up close and personal."

Shannon nods. "Me too."

"Look at this one though. He's just as hot... damn," she says, pointing at another guy next to *Guns*.

Jesus, I can't believe they've got me calling him that too.

Emy turns to face me. "So, what do you say? Are you down or what? It'll be loads of fun."

I scrunch up my nose. "I guess it wouldn't hurt to tag along."

"Yes! That's my best friend! That's my best friend!" Emy says in a singsong voice. "I'm going to get us tickets tonight when I get home."

"Are you sure they're not sold out?" Shannon asks.

Emy smirks. "Oh, they are. They've been sold out for a while now, but I've got connections."

"You do?" My brows furrow.

Emy flashes me a wide, open grin. "I do."

I can't wait to hear all about how she has connections to an event that's been sold out. "Do tell."

"Yes, Em. Do tell," Shannon repeats.

Emerson takes a sip from her glass, bats her eyes, and says, "I happen to personally know one of the guys fighting in the event."

My eyes go wide. "You do?"

Shannon grabs Emy's sleeve. "And you didn't tell us before? Oh, is it Guns? Is it Guns? Tell me it's Guns!"

Emy and I laugh.

Emy points at the man standing next to Guns. Jesus. I did it again. I shake my head.

"See this piece of eye candy right here, standing to the right of Guns? This is Ryker Manzoni, and I met him the other night. He was handing out these flyers at the mall. We struck up a conversation, and well, let's just say we hit it off nicely. If we want it, we're in."

"Ryker Manzoni? Jesus Christ. Even his name sounds hot," Shannon says.

"Doesn't it?" Emy taps on the one named Ryker three times. "Yum, yum, yum. I can't wait to see what he does inside the ring."

I have a feeling this is going to be a very interesting event.

The two of them carry on in a full-blown conversation about the men who will be fighting in the matches, but all I can do is wonder about the man who had stormed out of here. Where the hell had I seen him before?

Chapter Six

LORENZO

For the past week, all I've been seeing every night as I lie in bed and close my eyes are those same red luscious lips.

Luscious Lips. Fuck, she was something like I've never seen before. Her long dark curls, cascading down her back… her big brown eyes, and her amazing curves…

Wow. She was something else.

And yeah, I'm still referring to her as Luscious Lips. I seriously can't get those plump, crimson, heart-shaped puckers and the way they wrapped around that candy cane out of my mind. Fuck, it's been too long since I've gotten laid.

I need to snap out of my thoughts. This isn't the time or the place. I'm supposed to be focusing on my daughter, but I know she's in good hands.

I shake my head and lean back farther into the plastic chair connected to the table. I watch as Gianna laughs and plays with Marianna at the Skee-Ball machine.

It's crazy how much a tiny person can resemble the love of your life. The way her head whips back as laughter escapes her throat, with a twinkle in her eyes, reminds me so much of Sylvia, it hurts. She's got her same sparkling blue eyes.

Tears well in my eyes, and I casually bring up a hand to wipe them away.

"You all right, man?" Max asks, then stuffs a mouthful of cheesy pizza down his throat. It's been a week since our little altercation. I knew it wouldn't last long. We're family and very close-knit. Plus, we've had the same argument time and time again. I always end up coming to my senses and forgiving him. I know it's not his fault. I know he—as well as the rest of my family—want to see me happy and settled down again someday. I know they're tired of seeing me hurt. I can't blame them for caring. It's what they're supposed to do. I love them for it. Sometimes I just start missing Sylvia so much, all I want to do is fight anyone who says I should move on. Fuck moving on. I'll always love my wife. It was the promise I made her on the day we got married.

No. Scratch that. I promised I would love her for the rest of my life long before we were wed.

Anyone who suggests moving on always gets my blood boiling, and I'm instantly ready to fight them. It's the reason I joined the UFC after all, to get my frustration out and not have to take it out on the poor fucker.

Moving on is not an option. But moving forward, maybe.

I turn to face him. "Yeah, yeah. All good. I was just thinking—"

He nods. "How much she looks like Sylvs," he states more so than asks, turning his chin up toward where Gianna is playing. "I know. I was thinking it too."

"Is that normal? Five years later, and I still tear up every time I think about her like that?"

He takes a sip of his drink and says, "Of course, Enz. She was your wife. I think it's perfectly normal."

I take his words into consideration. Maybe he's right. Maybe I'm being too hard on myself, thinking something is wrong with me. We were together for so long, of course it still hurts.

Five years is not long when you spent just about half your life with someone who meant so much to you.

Five years is barely brushing the surface of a life together.

Max takes another bite of his pizza and swallows the mouthful. To this day, I still don't know how he likes Chuck E. Cheese pizza. To me, it tastes like frozen, reheated garbage. It's not my fault. I grew up on my mama's good, homemade Italian cooking. We both did, but my brother was a pain with food growing up. He was picky as hell. When we wanted pizza, she made it from scratch. Call me spoiled, but it's just the way it was—the way it still is whenever I go home.

I don't know what's wrong with my brother. We grew up in the same household, but seeing the way he eats this shit, you would never think so.

I scrunch my nose, making a face, then turn away from him to look at my daughter. She's still having a grand ole time with my sister. A smile pulls at the corners of my lips. Thank God for my baby girl. At least she's always able to melt my heart and make me smile.

I try to spend a lot of my free time with Gianna on my own, but tonight when we were heading out the door, she begged me to call Auntie Mari & Uncle Maxy.

Maxy... like a woman's maxi pad. I laugh at the funny name she'd given him.

"What's with the face, dude?" Max asks.

I turn back to face him. "What face?"

"The face you gave me before you looked away just now."

I hide a smile and look away. "I don't know what you're talking about, dude."

"Yeah, you do." He smirks. "You're grossed out because I'm eating this good, delicious pizza, aren't you?" It's not the first time we've had this same discussion.

"It's barf-worthy."

His eyes widen as he gasps. "It's delicious, all-American goodness."

"Nonna must be rolling around in her grave," I say jokingly, remembering how our grandmother hated anything that wasn't home cooked.

"Hey! Don't you bring Nonna into this."

I laugh and so does he.

After a moment, his expression changes to serious. "Look, man. I know we've already spoken about this and put it past us, but I'm really sorry about last week at Bottoms Up. I wasn't trying to insinuate you should ever forget about Sylvs. I know you miss her, and you're entitled to feel however you do. I just worry about you and Gianna, man. I want to see you guys happy."

I offer my brother a genuine smile so he knows I'm not harboring any hard feelings against him. "Max, I know. It's okay, really. I know it's not what you meant or were even trying to say. I know you care about me and Gianna. I'm not mad. I just overreacted that night. My temper got the best of me… You know how I am."

"My brother, the hothead," he says, smiling.

"Like you're not." I shake my head and take a sip of my drink.

"Daddy!"

I snap my head to the left and see my little princess running toward me at full speed. Marianna is trying to keep up behind her.

I instantly rise from my seat, and right before she's about to crash into me, I lift her up by her arms and spin her around above my head.

She shrieks and squeals, making me laugh. She's so precious.

As I spin us back around to our starting point, I bring her to me and place a kiss on her cheeks.

I place her on the ground. "Are you having fun, princess?"

"Oh, yes, Daddy! Aunt Mari is the best!"

"Hey, what about me?" Max feigns disappointment, but I know it's all a ploy to get Gia to run to him. He does this all the time.

"You don't count," Marianna states, finally reaching us.

I laugh.

"You're the best too, Uncle Maxy!" Gianna runs over and scoots in next to Max. He wraps his arms around her, and off they go chatting into their own little world. These two definitely have their own little bond, but I know that in her eyes, no one compares to Daddy. My little girl is very attached to me and loves me to the moon and back, same as me toward her.

Marianna and I take a seat across from Gianna and Max. Pouring the fruit punch into each of their cups, I lift my eyes for a second and see Gianna lay her head against Max's chest. I flick my wrist to get a look at my watch and realize it's about time to go home.

"Someone's getting ready to head to La La land." I take a sip from my cup before refilling it like I just did theirs. It's still cold and not too diluted, even though the ice melted a while ago.

"She plays hard," Marianna states. "Tonight was no exception. She gave me a run for my money."

We chuckle.

"That's cause you suck, Mari," Max says.

She smirks. "Hahaha. Very funny. A-s-s," she says, spelling it so Gianna doesn't pick up on it. This is what they do whenever they're bickering or playing around when my daughter's nearby.

"Oh, I'm an a-s-s, huh? Well, then you're an a-s-s l-i-c-k-e-r… and you can lick mine."

I try to hide a chuckle.

"No, thanks," Marianna retorts, closing her eyes and sticking out her tongue in disgust.

"Lick what?" Gianna lifts her head.

I give the two of them disapproving looks and then respond, "Ice cream, baby. Your aunt and uncle want some ice cream."

"Ooh, can I have some ice cream too, Daddy?" Her face lights up. It may be almost bedtime for my baby, but how can I say no to that face?

I smile at my princess. "Of course, baby. Let's get out of here and get some ice cream. And because your Uncle Maxy mentioned it, he can pay."

I smile widely at my brother as he playfully rolls his eyes. "Ice cream it is."

T he blaring alarm that sounds at 7:00 a.m. on Monday morning is like a bullet to my head. I spent all night tossing and turning, not being able to get comfortable and put my thoughts to rest.

Why is it that as soon as I close my eyes, bright-red lips are all I see?

I rise from my bed and head to the bathroom. It's still dark out, and I'd love to lie back down for another hour, but I'm not one to skip my morning routine. I relieve myself, brush my teeth, and head back to my bedroom to throw on some workout clothes and then head down the hall. I run for half an hour on the treadmill, trying to keep my focus on my heart rate and getting my laps in.

Once I'm done, I head back into the bathroom and jump in the shower.

By the time I'm done and had my first cup of coffee, it's time to wake up Gianna, drop her off at school, and get started with my errands.

But instead of coming home after dropping off my princess, I decide to head to training instead. With the big event coming up in a few days, I need to be in my best possible shape yet.

"You're here early," Ryker says as he sees me walking into the gym.

I shrug. "No time to waste. Figured I'd get it in early and maybe spend time with Gia after I pick her up instead of having my brother look after her. But anyways, so are you."

Ryker punches the bag in front of him a couple of times before responding. "I thought the same, but I haven't seen Mandy in a few days." He frowns. Mandy is his daughter. He's been broken up with her mother, Justine, for a little while now, and she doesn't make it easy for him to see her. I don't know why. He's a great dad, but she tries her best to give him a hard time. She's not that nice.

I consider asking about Mandy, but he's already back in the zone, and I don't want to further upset him.

I throw in my AirPods and select my workout playlist. I turn up the volume and take out some punches against the bag next to him. We continue in silence for the next twenty minutes.

"You ready for The Big Shot?" Ryker asks once we're done and in the locker room, getting changed.

I throw my gloves into my locker. "I've been ready. I've been dying to get my revenge and win that title once and for all." Dennis "The Big Shot" Mavis has been the only one standing in my way, and I intend on coming out on top next time we meet.

"You think you'll be all right?" he asks, lacing up his shoes.

I furrow my brows, giving him a look. "What do you mean?" And then it hits me. He's worried about me fighting on December fifth, just like Marianna was.

Ryker and I have been cool since I joined the UFC. I've kept my distance from pretty much everyone, but he's the only one besides my family whom I talk to and share my thoughts with. He knows all about Sylvia and Gianna.

I nod and take a seat on the wooden bench next to him. "Oh, yeah. Of course, man. I'll be fine."

The expression on his face tells me he's not convinced, but I pretend not to notice. I don't want to get into it right now. I need to get out of here.

"All right, man. I'll hit you up later," I say, rising from my seat. I throw my bag over my shoulder, and as I exit the locker room, I faintly hear him say, "I have a hard time believing it."

I exit the gym and head to my car. It's time to go pick up my princess.

Chapter Seven

CARISSA

I make my way to the breakroom, and upon entering, I pull out a chair and sit down. Today has been incredibly stressful, but I'm glad I get to take fifteen minutes to myself and not have to worry about patients or anything else.

Daniela marches in two minutes later, her cell phone in one hand and a Diet Coke in the other. Stomping and without meeting my gaze, she plops onto the seat next to mine. She's stressed out too. Today has definitely been challenging.

I met Daniela when I first started working here at the hospital a few years back. She was my first friend here, and since then, we've been fairly close. I either talk to her, Emy, or my sister, Shannon.

"I can't wait to get out of here," she says, placing her arms on the table and scrolling through her cell phone.

I nod. "Yeah, me too. It's definitely been a day."

She faces me. "*Definitely* been a day," she repeats. "What time do you get out tonight?" She places her phone onto the table and takes a sip of her Diet Coke.

"I'll be done by eight tonight. I've been here since early this morning."

"You pulled a double?" she asks, referring to my shifts, brushing her long blonde hair out of her face. "I did that yesterday. Couldn't do it again today. I'm drained, and I haven't even been here as long as you."

I shrug. "I need the money."

"Girl, you and me both. If I weren't so exhausted, I'd ask for them to let me stay longer and get that OT in. What's up for this weekend?"

This weekend? Ugh. I have been desperately trying not to think about it. Emy and Shannon are taking me to that fighting thing, but I still don't see a point in going. All it is, is a bunch of big muscled men going after one another like gorillas. How is that appealing? I'd rather stay home and read more of my romance novels. Those guys in my steamy love stories are the type of men I'd love to one day meet. Too bad none of them exist, and too bad I'm no longer looking to fall in love. I'm so done with all of it.

"Emy and Shannon are forcing me to go to some stupid fighting match in—"

"You mean the UFC fights on the fifth?" She sits up straighter with her eyes lighting up, cutting me off. Is she seriously as excited for the damn thing as my friend and sister are? What is it with these chicks?

I nod again. "Yeah, that's the one."

"Oh my God, girl! How the hell did you score tickets for that? I heard they've been sold out for a while now. My brother has been driving me crazy to go, but he hasn't been able to find a ticket."

Shrugging, I say, "Yeah, apparently Emy has connections."

She swallows another mouthful and says, "Emy is awesome. You have to invite me the next time you guys go out. She cracks me up, and I definitely need me some of those connections too." She chuckles.

I roll my eyes playfully. "I don't understand why you girls are going crazy over some stupid matchup."

She gasps. "Woman, it's not *some stupid matchup*. It's the event of the year. It's the biggest tournament in all of the UFC. Have you seen any of their advertisements on TV?" She looks at me, waiting for an answer, but I don't have one for her.

When I shake my head no, she exclaims, "Oh my God, are you effing kidding me? Lorenzo Trevano is going to take on Dennis "The Big Shot" Mavis in the title match. You can't honestly tell me you haven't heard about it. It's the biggest event of the year. And Lorenzo? Ufff... girl, he's hot as hell."

I give her a blank expression. "Sorry, girl. I don't know who any of those guys are. Emy quickly showed me some flyer with a few guys in front." And the man in the middle of it was definitely good looking. Even I have to admit that. But I'll never tell them and give them the satisfaction. "But names? I have no idea."

She shakes her head. Obviously, she disapproves of my ignorance in this matter. "Girl, you're missing out on some serious heartthrobs. These men are hot like fire! I can't wait to see them when they're all hot, sweaty, and shirtless. Fucking yum... Anyway, just go to the website. There's all their profiles on there. Some of them are so gorgeous."

Instantly, Guns's image from the poster Emy had shown me comes to my mind once more.

I did it again. Dammit, this is all Shannon and Emy's fault. This name has gotten stuck in my head. Every time I think about him, it's what I've been calling him. I can't lie though. He does have an impressive set of biceps.

Shaking my head, I rise from my chair. "Yeah, I guess so. Anyway, I have to get back now... Time is already up."

"Damn, break time always flies," she responds. She rises from her chair and walks to the trash bin to throw away her empty can.

"It does. I'll catch you later, girl."

By the time I get home, I'm drained. All I want to do is lie down and not worry about a damn thing for the rest of the night. I don't even want to eat dinner.

I throw my keys and a stack of mail onto the kitchen table and make my way into my bedroom. I strip out of my clothes and change into a gray T-shirt and black pajama pants. After pulling out the hair tie from my hair, I throw it on top of my dresser and decide that even though I'm not all that hungry, I should probably eat a little something. Not necessarily something heavy, but something that would just be enough so I don't wake up at midnight, starving. The only thing I've eaten all day is a salad at lunch.

I head into the kitchen and walk straight toward the fridge. A leftover slice of pizza from last night sits on a plate on the second shelf, so I pull it out and place it on a baking sheet. My stomach growls. How did I go from not being hungry at all to starving? I set the oven to heat up, and after a few minutes, I place the tray inside it.

When the timer dings, I take my plate to the table. It's just after nine, and once I finish eating, I'm looking forward to doing nothing else. Maybe I'll see if I can drown myself in a good movie or, better yet, read in the bathtub.

I take my first bite, and as I chew, the doorbell sounds. It must be Emy. Sometimes she shows up here unexpectedly. I hope she's not going to beg me to go out tonight because there is no way anyone is going to pull me out of these comfy pajama pants.

I rise and walk to the intercom next to the door, then push the button to talk. "Yes?"

"Carissa? God, it's good to hear your voice."

My stomach does a flip and ends in a knot. I know that voice. I know the voice so damn well.

It can't be.

Pushing the talk button once more, I ask, "What are you doing here?"

"Please let me up. This won't take long."

I take a deep breath and push the other button on the intercom, unlocking the door.

I pace back and forth as I wait for him to knock on the door to my apartment. Why is he here now? What does he want?

Moments later, three raps on my door make me jump back. I steady myself and go to open it.

My heart pounds in my chest. Why is he here? I can't imagine what on Earth he wants. It's been too damn long without a single word and now this?

Pulling the handle back, I lower my eyes to the ground, take another deep breath, and allow him back into my life. I hope I don't regret this later.

"Carissa." His voice is barely above a whisper, but it's loud enough for me to hear it.

My eyes flit to take in his image. He still looks the same after all this time. I swallow thickly, not saying a word.

It doesn't matter because the next words are his. "Damn, you look good... I've missed you."

Can't say the same about you... "What are you doing here, Steve?" I finally ask, biting the bullet.

He smirks, probably because my questioning him is not something he was expecting. He probably thought I was going to immediately welcome him with open arms.

Sorry, buddy. That's so not happening. Not this time.

"Can I please come in, babe? I don't want to have this discussion in your hallway."

Why the hell is he calling me babe? I roll my eyes but nevertheless allow him to come into my apartment. I close the door behind him and stand a few feet away from it. I will keep my distance from him if it kills me. "Okay. You're

49

inside. Now what is this about? Please make it quick. I'm pretty tired."

"Can we sit down and talk on the couch?" he asks. What is with him? Not a single word from him in three years, and now all of a sudden and out of nowhere, he wants to talk? What about all those times right after he broke my heart when I begged him to talk to me and he wouldn't give me a second glance? What about that? I bet he doesn't remember any of it. *Prick.*

I take a deep breath. This is going to take all my patience. I roll my eyes and lead him into the living room. I don't even invite him to sit. Instead, I plop down on one end and look up at him. "Well?"

He shakes his head, and after a few moments, he takes a seat next to me. "Carissa, babe. I've been thinking."

Oh, you have? For once, you've been using the head attached to your neck as opposed to the one in your pants? That's a first.

"Okay?" I ask, urging him on.

He reaches out to grab my hand, but I flinch.

"What the hell are you doing?"

He gives me one of his famous smug grins that I used to love. It's the same smug grin he put on every single time right after I'd lie down on the bed and he'd crawl above me, hovering over me. Chills run down my spine at the memory.

"Damn, I'm sorry, love. I didn't mean anything. I just want to feel close to you."

My patience is running out, and I seriously want him out of my apartment.

I stand from the couch and cross my arms over my chest. His eyes roam the length of my body, and I can tell he is not taking me seriously at all. I need to stop this. "Steve, I need you to leave. Now."

He jumps up. "Hey, babe. I'm sorry. Please don't ask me to leave. I know I can make you happy. Please let me stay.

I furrow my brows. "Steve, what the hell are you doing? *Let you stay?* You need to leave here before I call the cops."

He looks around him, but his gaze lands on me once more. "I don't want to leave, and I don't want you to call the cops."

I tap my foot. "You don't? Okay, so what do you want, Steve?"

"I want you," he responds casually.

I can't believe what I'm hearing. "Me? After all this time... me? You wanted to be with your ex. Do you remember? You left me, *your fiancée*, for your ex, and then you didn't say a word to me for years. I think it's clear, as it was pretty clear the day you made your choice. It wasn't me."

"But it is you!" he says. He steps closer and grabs my hand in his.

I don't pull it away this time. I'm so dumbfounded by what he's telling me. I shake my head. "No, Steve. It wasn't me then, and it's not me now. I'm sorry, but you really have to get going now."

Pulling me harder, he forces me onto him until my mouth is inches from his.

The same mouth that once upon a time used to kiss me so sweetly.

The same mouth that once upon a time used to make me shudder with anticipation right before we'd give ourselves over to one another, becoming one in the middle of the night.

The same mouth that eventually spoke the words saying he no longer loved me and wanted to be with someone else, only months before we were set to be wed.

Bitter memories cloud my vision, but as I'm coming to, I gasp. "Steve, let me go!"

He chuckles wickedly. "You were mine then as you will always be mine and belong to me—when I want, and how I want. Don't you ever forget that." He whispers those last five words, and his breath is warm against my face. A sudden flashback to times he got drunk and grabbed me the way he just did flood my brain. It took me months after he left for me to realize that how he'd treated me was worse than I'd thought. This can't be happening all over again. I need to get away from him.

I desperately try to break away from his grasp, but I can't. He's too strong, and his grip on me is too tight.

One of his hands lands on my ass and he squeezes tightly. "You always did have such a nice round booty... Mmm, the things I want to do to it right now. Why don't we make our way to *our* bedroom, huh?"

"Fuck you!" I shout, trying desperately to break away from his hold. This is my place now. He no longer lives here. He grabs me from the waist and pulls me out of the living room and into the hallway. I grip onto the doorjamb and hold on as tightly as I possibly can, but my hands are slipping and hurting from gripping so tightly. "No!" I scream. "Let me go!"

"What's going on here?" A familiar voice I adore so much comes to my rescue. My eyes dash toward the front door. Thank God for the spare key only she and my sister know sits tucked behind the portrait hanging right outside the door.

Steve's grip on me immediately loosens at the distraction, and I stumble forward and move as far away from him as I possibly can. I run to my best friend's side. "Emy!" I wrap my arms around her, so thankful that she barged in and interrupted his ploy.

She gives me a once-over and asks, "Are you okay, girl?"

I nod. "Yeah, yeah. I'm fine." We let go of our embrace, and I stand next to her, hugging myself. I hate that he had his hands on me. I hate the memories that crashed back to my mind. It took me so long to move forward from all of it, his physical and emotional abuse and his cheating ways. And now, he's just brought it all back. I shudder. I feel dirty and can't wait to shower.

Turning to face Steve, she places a hand on her hip. "What the hell are you doing here, Steve?"

He puts on a smug grin, backing against the wall. "Emy. Figures you'd show up right when we were about to get to business. You always did know how to cock-block our relationship. It's *so* nice to see you again too."

She smirks. "Quit the smart remarks, ass clown. And thank God I did get here when I did because it appears as though you've overstayed your welcome. It's time for you to go. Or I'll call the cops."

Steve throws me a look and then glares back at my friend. "Call the cops? For what? For coming over to see my girl? Please…"

"I'm not your girl, Steve!" I roar. My blood is boiling, and now my fists are balled tightly at my sides. I refuse to let him treat me the way he used to. Not now, not ever again.

"You need to leave. Now," Emy responds.

He doesn't flinch, and Emy nods her head.

"Like I said, either you go or I'm calling the cops."

He crosses his arms, leaning against the wall. "You wouldn't."

Emy's eyes widen. "Oh, I wouldn't? Watch me." She pulls out her phone and hits the number nine.

It immediately makes Steve jump forward and stop her from dialing the rest of the digits. "Okay, fine, fine. I'm going." He walks toward us and then, looking at me directly in the eyes, he says, "But this isn't over, Carissa. We're not through."

"Good-bye, Steve," Emy exclaims, forcing him out.

As he leaves my apartment, I quickly lock the door behind him and stand with my back against it. I'm instantly met with Emy's disapproving glance. "What?"

She raises an eyebrow like The Rock. *"What?* You're joking, right? You don't know what I'm going to say?"

"I know. I'm sorry. I let him back in. I should be more careful," I reply.

She frowns and marches into the living room. I follow.

Pulling out her phone, she rolls her eyes and furiously types something into it.

"Who are you texting?" I ask.

When she's done moments later, she looks up at me. "Shannon."

"Shannon? Why the hell are you texting Shannon now?" I know why. She's going to tell her exactly what happened. *Fuck.*

Emy stands and crosses her arms across her chest. She lets out a deep exhale. "This could have ended so much worse than it did, Carissa. So much worse. I'm sorry, but I worry about you, and seeing him here after so long, knowing what he's capable of, really scared the crap out of me. You're my best friend, and the last thing I want is for some asshole like Steve to hurt you all over again."

I shrug. "I know. I just… I don't know what I was thinking. He said there was something he needed to talk to me about, so I lowered my guard."

She nods. "You're a good person, Carissa. And sometimes, that causes people to take advantage of you. Like Steve. Here he was with his hands on you all over again. If I would have gotten here one second later, God knows what could have happened or what I would have walked into. I love you, *chica.*"

I smile. "I love you too."

"What made you stop by anyway?" I ask.

Emy sits back down on the couch, and I take a seat across from her. "I was coming to drop off this." She pulls out a flyer for the upcoming event this weekend. It's a different one

54

from last time. The guys are now standing in the middle of the ring.

"Look. These are the brand new flyers going around." Throwing the flyer onto my coffee table, she smiles from ear to ear.

I lean closer to get a better look. "Okay… I'm not sure what you want me to see here besides the fact that it's a new flyer."

Rolling her eyes, she picks it up off the table and stands. She walks over to me, grabs me by the arm, and makes me stand. "Look again."

I take another glance at the flyer and then I see it. "Oh my God."

She giggles. "That's *him.* Guns's name is Lorenzo Trevano. It's written right here underneath his picture."

"Wait… it can't be—"

"Guns! It's Guns!" she exclaims. "*He's* the stud muffin from the bar the other night. What are the odds?"

I swallow thickly as images of him from the night at the bar come back to the front of my mind…

"No way…"

"Oh, yes way… look at this." She pulls out the first flyer from her pocket and places them side by side. The man from the bar the other night is Guns…

I take a moment to process my thoughts. "So he's going to be fighting this weekend at the matchup?" I obviously already know the answer because Daniela told me already, but I can't believe it. What a small world.

"Hang on," she says, bringing up her cell phone again. "Okay, Shannon's on her way to make sure you're all right after the little stunt Steve just pulled."

I shrug. "She really doesn't have to stop by."

She waves a dismissive hand in my direction. "But yes, he is in the main event, fighting The Big Shot this Saturday."

"Wow," I say, taking a seat again.

Emy sits next to me. "Yeah, and just think. We'll be there like two rows away, watching him up close."

I snap my head in her direction. "I don't think I—"

"Oh, hell naw, girl. I got tickets, and we're going. We're *so* going. Don't give Shannon and me another reason to beat you down. We've already got one."

"Great. I can't wait."

Chapter Eight

LORENZO

Anger flares deep in my veins. Every year on this day, it appears as though I never find peace. Instead, I'm angry and blaming the world for all that was robbed from me and my little girl. Why us? Why did we have to go through it? Why was Sylvia taken away from us?

But this kind of anger will allow me to do all I'm meant to do tonight. My broken heart and mess of a life will be the drive I need to accomplish my dreams.

In the middle of a crowded arena, I stand in a cage as the announcer is about ready to announce my name taking on Dennis "The Big Shot" Mavis. The commencement of the fight is about to be underway, and there is nothing better than it allowing rage to build inside me so I can take it out on my opponent. The day has finally come for me to take what officially belongs to me.

It's a day for revenge, and as I stand here in the center of the cage, I'm ready to let my inner beast out and let the havoc I feel inside take its place on Dennis "The Big Shot" Mavis's face. He's the only one standing in my way of being an undefeated champion and the one who currently holds the title.

But not for long. It's going to be mine, all mine, before the end of the night.

When the bell rings, alerting us it's go time, I stand across from Dennis, eyeing him down. He glares back at me, but I'm not intimidated by his two inches over me. I won't let up, and I refuse to let him think this is going to be easy, because I can guarantee that's one thing it's not going to be.

Almost immediately, he comes forward, lunging at me. I take shots into his sides as he does the same, but it doesn't matter. I keep punching and sending shots his way. I want this more. So much more.

He hasn't been through the things I've been through. He hasn't traveled the same journey as I have. He doesn't have the same drive and desire for wanting this as badly as I do.

It may take time and determination, but I'm not giving up until I come out on top.

A blow meets my jaw, causing blood to gush out and onto the floor. It doesn't stop me. It doesn't even slow me down. All it does is make me angrier, allowing me to channel my energy into a shot of my own, and it connects with his face.

A fter three rounds, each lasting no longer than five minutes of us going completely berserk and beast mode on one another, the match finally comes to an end. I've got a swollen black eye, but nothing can compare to the ecstatic and victorious way I'm feeling.

The crowd is going wild, cheering and applauding as the announcer lifts my right hand into the air and announces me as the heavyweight champion. I've been training for this night for months, and it finally paid off. The belt around my waist is the confirmation that this moment is indeed mine to enjoy.

As the applause and cheers grow louder and louder and

the reality that I've won hits home, everything slowly goes silent. The cheering crowd is still going, but I can't hear a thing. The lights dim, and the only person I see, sitting two rows away, is *her*.

Luscious Lips.

She's here and she's cheering for me, standing next to two of her friends. Her shimmering smile has my heart feeling as though it's skipped a beat. God, she's breathtaking. I can't believe she's here. And she's smiling at me, cheering away with the rest of the crowd.

Her big, brown eyes sparkle brightly. Her hair is pinned up halfway, and a red blouse snuggly hugging her breasts sits on top of jeans. I no longer feel the pain from the injured body parts where Dennis got me. The pounding headache, the pulsating cuts on my face, and my aching joints no longer bother me. Everything has gone still and silent. The only thing I feel is my heartbeat, which is gripping the hold of my attention on her.

I'm not sure how much time passes, but at some point, our coaches and Ryker barge into the ring, shouting and celebrating my win. I'm ripped away as they lead me out of the arena, but my eyes never leave hers.

Lying in bed, hours after a celebration at a nearby diner, I'm finally able to relax and get some rest. My baby girl is staying with my parents this weekend. They knew whether I'd win or lose that it would be a late night, so they kept her entertained at home while Max and Marianna cheered me on at the match.

I wouldn't trade tonight for anything. It was all amazing, and the fact that I saw her again and our eyes met really put the icing on the cake.

I frown.

What's wrong with me? It's the anniversary of Sylvia's passing, and here I am lying in bed not able to get some random woman out of my head. I flip over to the other side. Ow. The pain. I adjust the ice pack and hope it rids my thoughts of Luscious Li—

Okay, I need to stop that too. I can't keep calling her *that* any longer. I wish I knew her name so I can refer to her as it instead.

Fuck it, I'm going to call her Lush. That's better, right?

Mmm… maybe. I don't know. I still picture the way her lips wrapped around that candy cane the first night, and oh my God, I'm getting hard.

Fuck! Stop it!

This isn't happening.

Maybe I need to relieve myself. I mean, with the match and training, I have been pretty tied up and exhausted by the time I get into bed. Maybe if I just jerk off, I can end this craziness and forget about this woman once and for all.

Yes, that's exactly what I'm going to do. I hope I don't regret this because I'm really sore right now, but I have to try to get these thoughts out of my head one way or another.

I carefully turn to lie onto my back. After gently kicking the blankets off myself, I reach down slowly to my boxer briefs and lower them as well. Okay, the pain is not so bad. My cock springs free, aching for some relief. *Damn.*

From inside the bottom drawer of the nightstand, I pull out a pair of socks and separate them. I reach down and palm my hard cock, and it increases in size. Fuck, it's been too long.

I stroke it only a couple of times, but it still feels fucking good. I need to come. I place one of my socks over it.

Once it's on, I work my length up and down, trying to think about the sensation so I can reach my pleasure zone. But instead of being able to focus on how good it is to feel it being jerked up and down, Lush's face comes into view, and I picture her lips wrapped around my cock, like she was doing to that candy cane. Fuck, she's so damn sexy. Her hooded eyes look up at me as she alternates between sucking on my dick and licking up and down the length of it.

Fuck, I can't control it. Thinking about her in that position with me in her mouth makes me completely lose it, and moments later, I'm exploding into my sock.

Wow… That was intense.

Guilt burdens me instantly after.

This can never happen again.

It should have never happened in the first place. But now that it's over with I've gotten *her* out of my system, I should be fine. I just needed some relief. I am a man, after all.

I pull the sock off my dick slowly and carefully, as to not let the come drip out, and then place it carefully on my nightstand. I'll throw it in the bin full of dirty laundry in the morning.

I toss over to the other side and curse. Fuck… I'm sore as hell. I need to be more careful when I move and take my time. I take a deep breath and close my eyes, but when I do, all I see is her.

Chapter Nine

CARISSA

"Okay, girl... all the hot juicy details? I want them! I want them all, and don't you *dare* skip over anything!" Daniela urges me to tell her all about my evening Saturday night at the MMA fight.

It's Monday morning, and as soon as I arrived at the hospital, she started hounding me to tell her about it. It's not like there's really anything to tell though.

Well, that's besides the fact that Lorenzo "Guns" Trevano is now my absolute favorite name. God, he was fire on Saturday, and I was ice being melted away by his stare.

No, this doesn't change my mind about all men being scum. Just because I'm starting to feel a little crush toward this hot man doesn't mean I would ever date him—or anyone else for that matter. I have no intention of falling in love ever again. I plan to remain single for the rest of my life. At least this way it's a sure thing of not getting my heart broken all over again.

We take a seat after entering the breakroom, and before I can take a bite of my pretzel, I look her in the eyes and say, "Guns is fine."

I don't even know where I got the courage to blurt that out, but somehow I did.

"Who's Guns?" she asks, eyes wide.

I bite down on my bottom lip. Of course she doesn't know who Guns is. It's a nickname my sister and my friend gave him. "Lorenzo Trevano."

"Oh my God! I know! He's so hot! That face and that body? Uff… Makes me hot just thinking about him." She fans herself.

I chuckle. "He is very gorgeous, and I can't believe I'm even saying it."

"Hey, there's nothing wrong with admiring a fine-looking man. And Guns?" she asks.

I shrug. "It's the nickname Emerson and Shannon gave him. They started referring to him as that so much because of the size of his biceps. I automatically adopted it, without even trying. Now it just comes out."

She smirks. "Well, shit. It suits him."

"I still can't believe he had the balls to come in here after everything. Like, you guys were engaged, ready to be married, and he goes and sleeps with his ex? Makes no sense to me." Shannon sits across from me at the kitchen table in my apartment. Yeah, we're talking about this again while we wait for Emy to meet us here in a few minutes.

I shrug. "It wasn't as though that was the first time he did it. When I caught him, he came clean about being with her multiple times in the past. He really killed my ability to trust someone. I loved him with all my heart. I never imagined he'd do this to me."

She pops a chip into her mouth, and after chewing and swallowing, she responds. "I know. Which is why I'm surprised he came by."

I nod. "And after so long."

"Had he called or texted you before showing up?"

I shake my head. "Nope, not even a text."

"And it's not like you ever changed your number since you two broke up."

I sip on a glass of water. "Nope, it's been the same this whole time."

Of course, after we first broke up, I thought of changing my number. But then, after a couple of days of him not even bothering to reach out, I figured there was no point. He didn't even try apologizing or talking to me. So I left it at that. If I had changed it, I might have thought he tried to call me before stopping by the other day.

But does it even matter?

"What's up, bitches!" Emy's voice booms through the apartment. "I brought goodies!"

"We're in the kitchen," Shannon calls.

Moments later, Emy walks in, her hands full of brown paper bags. She places them onto the table.

"What's in the bags?" I ask.

Emy looks at me with a wide-open smile. "Goodies."

"Yeah, we heard you say that, but *what kind* of goodies?" Shannon asks.

Emy's smile widens. "The kind of goodies sure enough to get us fucked up and make us happy."

"That's my girl," Shannon states, helping Emy pull out two bottles of Ciroc and a bottle of Moscato from the paper bags.

I roll my eyes and laugh. "But of course. You know I'm not crazy about drinking."

"Who do you think these are for?" Emy asks, pulling out a box of Entenmann's cookies and a bottle of frozen iced coffee.

"Iced coffee! My savior!" I grab the bottle from her. I couldn't care less about the cookies.

"Emy Claus delivers," she answers with a wink.

Shannon laughs. "Emy Claus, that's a good one."

Emy walks toward the cupboard above the counters and pulls out two wine glasses, then walks them to the table and takes a seat. After pouring some Moscato into her glass, she takes her first sip. "Damn, that's good and so fucking needed after a day at work."

"Girl, yes. And especially after the conversation I just had with this one." Shannon points at me with her right thumb.

"Oh, come on." I hate that I'm the topic of discussion… *again.*

"Oh, shit. What conversation did I miss?" Emy asks and takes another sip.

Shannon grabs a glass from the table and fills it with Moscato. "Steve the Ass."

Emy's eyes widen. "Ah… Steve the Ass. This conversation also wouldn't have anything to do with his little stunt I had to break up the other day?"

"It sure would," Shannon answers.

Okay, so maybe now I do care about the cookies. I flip open the box and grab a handful. "It wasn't my fault."

"Not at all," Emy answers. "But you should have never let him in."

"Right, girl," Shannon says.

I look away from them, stuff cookies into my mouth, and chew. "Can we change discussion… please."

Emy laughs. "Sure, chunky cheeks. Let's talk about Guns. Or should I say *Lorenzo Trevano.*"

I immediately dart my eyes in her direction at the mention of his name.

"Yeah, I thought that would grab your attention," Emy says.

I throw her a questioning stare. "And what's that supposed to mean?"

Shannon giggles to herself and chugs another mouthful of wine.

Emy sits back in her seat. "Oh, nothing... except that you are finding it hard to keep your mind off of him."

How the hell does she know? I guess she's my best friend for a reason, but damn. I hadn't said as much.

"I bet she wouldn't mind keeping something else off of him," Shannon says, and the two of them start cracking up.

I glare at her, crumpling up a napkin, and throw it her way. "Shut up, witch."

But deep down inside, I know she's right.

I push my cart into aisle five: baking supplies. Shannon's birthday is tomorrow, and I'm planning on making her a birthday cake. Red velvet cheesecake.

Cheesecake. Cream cheese. I'd better go grab some before I forget. I need to head to the dairy section of the grocery store. I always leave that aisle for last because every time I'm there, I freeze. It totally doesn't help that I'm wearing a miniskirt right now. Like what had possessed me?

Emy is supposed to be coming over for dinner, and afterward, we're planning to head out. Shannon can't make up her mind on whether she wants to go to the movies or go dancing. I'm hoping she picks the movies because I really don't want to go dancing, but it is her birthday, and I will sacrifice what I need to make her happy.

I push my cart into the dairy section and scan the items. Yogurt... butter... mozzarella... cream cheese. Bingo.

Reaching to grab it, my hand brushes against another as it tries to grab the same thing.

I snap my head to the left and... holy shit. What are the odds? Out of all the freaking places to be on a typical weekday afternoon... How?

Lorenzo "Guns" Trevano is here, shopping at the same freaking grocery store as me. I'm surprised he doesn't have people to shop for him.

"Oh, I'm sorry," I say, pulling back. My heart speeds and my hands tremble. I can't believe he's standing so close to me.

A warm smile forms on his face. "No, no. It's my fault. Please, go ahead."

I smile back, unable to withhold it. Slowly, I reach forward and grab two containers of cheese, still staring at him.

His smiling face turns into a puzzled expression. "That's a lot of cream cheese," he says. "Planning brunch for a big crowd?" Now he's smiling again.

Suddenly realizing that I was grabbing more cheese off the shelf, I quickly stop. Somehow, two containers of cream cheese became four, four became five, and finally six. In no time, I had managed to clear the store of their entire stock of cream cheese by putting them all in my basket.

I feel my cheeks turning bright red. Way to embarrass yourself, Carissa.

"Oh, fu—" I catch myself before letting out the obscenity. "I'm sorry…" I begin placing the containers of cream cheese back.

He chuckles and holds out his hands to show he's not offended. "May I?" he finally asks, pointing at the containers still in my hands, asking if he can have one.

"Oh, yes, of course!" I pass one to him. "You want more?"

He chuckles again. "No, no. One is quite enough, thanks." He places it into his cart.

Of course it is, Carissa, you moron.

Who goes out to clear the supermarket of their entire stock of cream cheese? Only me. I place all but two of the containers back onto the shelf.

"I've seen you around before... I'm Lorenzo," he says in a cool, sultry voice, extending his hand.

I reach and grab it. Holy fuck, what a grip. His hand is like twice the size of mine... maybe more. I don't know, but my tiny one gets swallowed by his much larger one.

I nod. "Yes, I saw you at the match the other night. I'm Carissa. Nice to meet you."

Now he nods and then our hands let go.

But our eyes don't. We don't let go of one another's gaze, and I'm beginning to feel uncomfortable... self-conscious.

Shit, is my hair in place? Is this shirt too tight? Ugh... I hate questioning myself right now and feeling this way.

His eyes are completely eating me whole, and it seems like he's staring at... my lips? Fuck, is my lipstick smeared? I want to pull out my pocket mirror from my purse, but it would be too obvious.

Okay, I need to take a deep breath and relax. I need to cool off. I need to remind myself he's just another guy.

Another guy who is most likely another asshole.

Shit, a guy like him probably has women hanging all over him on a daily basis. He's sure to be a complete heart-breaking asshole. They're all the same, and I'm sure he's as cocky, arrogant, and dick-headed as they all are.

I've had more than my share of it all, and I'm not looking for another way to get my heart broken.

I need to keep my cool and remind myself that all guys are no good. All guys are pricks only looking for one thing.

He breaks my train of thought with his next words. "Well, I don't mean to hold you up. I'm sure you have places to be." He pauses for a second, staring at my mouth again for a bit too long. "It was nice officially meeting you, Carissa."

Damn, the way he said my name...

Nodding, I respond, "Likewise."

Our eyes continue to take one another in, but something deep inside me is causing heat to form deep in my core.

Fuck, he's hot. His smoldering look, burning into me... his sexy grin... He's igniting a fire within me I'm not sure I can control.

Dammit, Carissa. Get your shit together. Focus...

Remember, he's no good for you. He's an asshole, only looking for one thing.

Okay, sure, all guys are pricks, assholes, and shitheads only looking for one thing, but something about the way he bores his gaze into me is making it really hard for me to follow the rules I set aside for myself.

Chapter Ten

LORENZO

"Where's Jordan?" I ask my sister as we're sitting around the dining room table enjoying Mom's Sunday dinner. He had finally reached out to her a few days ago and was supposed to be here with us today. It's tradition for the family to be here on Sundays, but it's not the first one he's missed.

Marianna shrugs, failing to meet my gaze. "Away on business again."

Shit. My sister's husband is constantly away on business, or so he says. I don't know if it's true, and I know my sister is skeptical about it as well. It's a touchy subject, but for his sake, it better be true. I'll kill him if he hurts her.

"Ma, this rigatoni-and-sausage combo is amazing," Max says, chiming in, and I'm thankful for the change in topic.

"Uncle Maxy... that's a lot of food in your mouth."

I look over at my five-year-old who has dropped her fork and is looking to her right. She's staring wide-eyed at her Uncle Maxy scarfing down his plate of pasta.

I chuckle to myself and lean down to whisper in her ear. "And just think... When your uncle was your age, all he ate was mac and cheese. He never wanted to eat Grandma's food."

"But it's so good," she answers back quietly.

"What are you whispering to her?" Max looks at me, with a raised eyebrow.

"I know, right?" I say to her. Straightening back up, I take a glance at Max again. "Oh, so I guess now your mouth is empty enough to speak." I chuckle again. "I wasn't saying anything false. I was just telling her you used to always pass up Mom's food when we were kids. Thankfully, she can't believe it because she knows it's delicious, even at her age. I have to say my five-year-old's a whole lot smarter than you were back then... well, now too." I snicker.

"You kids never quit," my father says after swallowing a mouthful of red wine. Then, looking at his little grand-daughter sitting to his left, he says, "It's okay, sweetheart. Don't pay them no mind. There are three bites left on your plate. Eat up." He winks at her.

Gianna's dumbfounded expression quickly changes. She smiles, picks her fork back up, and resumes stuffing another bite of pasta into her mouth. For a kid, she eats rather well and rarely complains when she's served something she doesn't recognize. Whenever my mother cooks for her, Gianna always cleans the plate.

"Enz was telling Gia what a moron you are," Marianna states from the opposite side of the table, looking at Max.

"That's enough, you guys!" Mom walks into the dining room carrying yet another plate full of food. This time it's chicken cutlets, potatoes, and stuffed and roasted red peppers.

All I can say is that Sunday dinners at my parents' house are the best. Mom always makes sure we don't ever run out of food. I leave here ten pounds heavier than I was when I arrived.

"Ooh, Ma. Let me help," Marianna says, rising from her

seat. She picks up empty dishes from the table to make room for the second part of dinner. The first dish is always some type of pasta. The second part is usually a type of meat, followed by whatever side dishes Mom decides to make. Her stuffed and roasted red peppers are to die for.

Marianna walks to Gianna, whose plate is now completely polished. Like I said, she never leaves food behind when my mother cooks.

"Good girl!" Marianna leans down and kisses the top of Gianna's head. She takes her plate away and continues clearing the first round of dishes.

As soon as Marianna has swiped our finished plates from the table, Mom places new ones onto the middle of it. "Here we are."

Max is first to fork a cutlet and place it onto his plate.

I shake my head but don't make a comment. Unfortunately, my brother never did know how to let things go when it came to messing with me. You would think he would be wiser than to pick on me, since I am larger than him, but as kids, we wrestled all the time because of his mouth. I only let him win once, when I felt bad for him. His bike got stolen by some of the neighborhood kids. It was a sweet bike, one he had been wanting for months before my parents gave in and bought it for him for his birthday. While he was sad about it all day long, it didn't stop him from starting a name-calling competition with me. I can't remember what it was over, but most likely, it was what to watch on TV or whose turn it was to take out the trash.

As we were messing around one night after dinner, picking on one another, I let him believe I wasn't able to win a match of arm wrestling. He was none the wiser, and I left it alone. It doesn't need to be said that I got his bike back from those kids. It was the last time they ever messed with my brother.

Max, noticing I'm purposely watching him, places his

fork down. "I am the middle child. Because of this, I get first dibs on Ma's food."

"That makes absolutely no sense, Max," Marianna states as she fills her glass with wine.

Max nods and smiles. "Enz knows what I mean."

My eyebrows narrow. "Sorry, Max. I have no clue as to what you're referring to. I have to agree with Marianna. That makes no sense whatsoever."

He rolls his eyes and smirks. "Growing up, I always had to make sure I got what was deserved. The oldest gets this and the youngest gets that. What about the middle child?"

"Massimo, you and Marianna are twins. There is no middle child," my dad states, never lifting his gaze from his dish.

I chuckle. "Dad told you. Now shut up and eat."

"There was *too* a middle child, and it was me!" Max exclaims.

"Cool your shorts, Massimo. Eat," Mom states.

At this point, Gianna, Marianna, and I are cracking up.

My brother, refusing to relent, looks at me and says, "Don't worry, big bro. In a few more years, Mother Nature will be my payback."

Furrowing my brows yet again, I ask through a chuckle, "What the hell are you talking about?"

Quickly realizing what I've said, I shoot Mom a look, who is now glaring at me. "Watch your language, mister."

I shrug. "Sorry, Ma."

Max speaks again and points at Gianna without grabbing her attention. "Big blue eyes, gorgeous long, flowing curls… She's going to be a heartbreaker, for sure. All the little boys will be lined up outside your house, waiting to take her out."

This realization has dawned on me many times, but I always quickly threw it out of my head. I know my little girl is going to have guys calling her, asking to go out with her, but it's not something I'm looking forward to—and not something I think I will ever be ready for.

Gianna is my little girl, my princess. These *little boys* my brother is referring to better look the other way and keep it moving. Her daddy doesn't play. I'm ready to kill the first guy who tries anything with my baby.

Marianna cuts in before I have a chance to speak. "Yeah, and you'll be standing right next to Enz with Dad, and the three of you will be holding rifles, scaring off those poor boys."

"Ain't that the truth," Mom says, giggling.

Marianna nods. "Ma and I will be desperately trying to calm her down. She's got an old-school Italian grandpa, a crazy uncle, and an ill-tempered daddy who are going to embarrass her on more than one occasion, I'm sure."

"It's in her best interest that people know not to break her heart," I say.

"Break her heart, or even look at her?" Max asks.

I smirk. "They'd better not look at her."

"And that's the truth," Mom says, laughing again as she takes a seat to my dad's right.

Gianna tugs on my sleeve. "Daddy, what are you guys talking about?"

I smile down at my baby girl who's oblivious to it all, and I'm so thankful for that right now. "Nothing, sweetheart. Eat up. We have to get going soon. You have school tomorrow."

"K," she answers and stabs a potato with her fork. Moments later, she tugs on my sleeve again.

"Yes, princess?"

"Can we get a mistletoe?"

My eyebrows narrow. "Mistletoe?"

"Yes! We decorated some at school on Friday. Please, Daddy! Can we?"

Max's laughter causes me to look at him once more.

"Mistletoe means kisses. It's starting, bro. Like I said, Mother Nature will soon take its course. Payback, Enz. Payback." He makes a kissing face at me.

I scowl.

Marianna intervenes. "Payback for who, Bozo? I already told you, you're going to be feeling it too, the day she gets boys calling her. It's going to be payback for all three of the Trevano men," Marianna says.

I laugh. Marianna's got a point. When that dreaded day comes, the three of us are going to be standing right behind my little girl, making sure there's no funny business. Those boys will think twice before they try anything.

I lean down and place a kiss on my baby's head. "Yes, sweetheart. We can get a mistletoe for our house."

After Gianna and I get home, I give her a bath and tuck her into bed. She's out after fifteen minutes of me reading her favorite fairytale to her: *Snow White*.

I leave the door to her room cracked open and walk out into the living room. I contemplate jogging off all the food I ate at Mom's on the treadmill, but I don't think I can right now. I'd probably vomit. I decide to hit the sack instead and watch TV until I pass out. I hate being lazy, but I don't want to get sick.

I strip out of my clothes and change into a plain white T-shirt and a pair of plaid pajama pants. I climb into bed, lying on top of my comforter. If my mother could see me, she'd yell at me right now, saying I'll mess up the quilt. She has a thing about comforters. I always thought they were meant to be used any way to be comfortable, hence the word *comfort* in them, but Mom seems to believe something else. I chuckle to myself and flip through some channels.

Once I feel myself start to doze off, I climb out of bed and remove my shirt. That alarm is going to sound before I know it, so I'd better try to get some sleep. I toss the pants to the side, so they land on the chair to the right of my bed, and pull the covers down.

Climbing back into bed, I find a comfortable position. Then I set the TV on a timer to turn off, and I close my eyes.

Tonight's dinner conversation plays over in my mind. My brother is hilarious. If he thinks Gianna's growing up is not going to have any effect on him, he's got another thing coming. I remember the way he was so sure of himself when he moved the container of parmesan cheese—

Cheese.

Cream cheese.

Carissa… Luscious Lips.

No, I have to stop associating that phrase with her whenever I think about her. I know her name now, so no more calling her Luscious Lips, or Lushy, or anything of the sort.

What the hell am I saying, *whenever I think about her?* I need to stop thinking about her right now.

Damn, I was so close to not thinking about her all day. I kept my mind preoccupied the whole time so I wouldn't have to think about our little chance encounter at the super-market the other night, but I failed.

Now all I can see are her big brown eyes, perfect smile, and, of course, luscious lips.

Fuck, I'm in so much trouble. Now that I've seen her at the supermarket, I wonder if I'll be running into her a lot more. If I do, I'm screwed.

But the truth is… I want to see her.

I hate to admit it. The way I've been feeling lately is making me feel like a horrible husband to my wife.

But she's gone. Sylvia is gone and has been for five years now. When is it okay to start over? When is it okay to love again—or perhaps not even love, but date?

I flip to the other side, now lying toward my nightstand. I hate the fact I'm even thinking this way. It feels so wrong.

But Carissa makes me feel things I haven't felt in so damn long.

I open my eyes, and the first thing I see is a picture of Sylvia from so long ago. I frown. "I'm so sorry, Sylvs."

Chapter Eleven

CARISSA

"Seriously, seventy-five dollars... for a damn oil change? Something's not right. That seems stupid high. I don't know; I wouldn't do it. No. No, go to my mechanic. I'll text you his info. His prices are very competitive, and he's a hell of a mechanic. Yup. Yes, that's him. Uh huh, that's right. The owner. Very good with his hands, and he's hot as hell. No, I wish! I think he's married or something. Because the last time I was there, I noticed some pictures he has on the wall. But yeah, go visit him. He'll give you a nice deal. Okay, I'll see you tonight. Okay, bye." Emy hangs up the phone before swinging her legs over the side of the couch to get comfortable.

"What was that about?"

She shrugs. "My cousin's car needed an oil change. She took it to the mechanic herself since her boyfriend's out of town, and he wanted to charge her an arm and a leg."

I nod. "Yeah, I heard."

Emy picks up her cell phone and scrolls through it. "I told her to go visit my mechanic. Uff... he's fine."

I chuckle. "I picked up on that too."

She smiles up at me. "The next time I go, I'm taking you with me so you can see for yourself."

I furrow my brows. "What's the point?"

She scoffs. "Of course you would say that."

"I'm just saying. Even if I were looking"—I make a stern face—"which I'm not, so let me make that perfectly clear… you said so yourself he was taken."

She throws a dismissive hand in my direction. "Blah, blah. So what?"

I shake my head.

"Oh, that's right. You've still got Mr. Guns on your mind." She chuckles.

I hate myself right now for even mentioning the little encounter we had a few days ago at the supermarket, but I had to tell someone. The way he looked at me and the way he was making me feel? I just couldn't keep it to myself.

Of course, when I told her, Shannon had been there too. Now my sister is at work, while Emy and I are sitting in her apartment, wrapping presents for Christmas in a few weeks. Emy has quite a few nieces and nephews. Her mother had six kids in total: three daughters and three sons. Emy is the youngest, and of all of Mrs. Lexington's children, Emy is the only one who hasn't had any kids.

"Think Jayla is going to like this one?" Emy holds up a doll dressed in a pink-and-white ensemble. Jayla is one of her younger nieces and is probably the most spoiled of them all by Emy, since she lives close by. A lot of her family lives across the country.

I'm so thankful for the change in topic. I really don't want to talk about me and my supermarket adventure with Guns.

I nod. "She's princess pink. She's going to love that."

Emy smiles. "I can't wait to see the huge smile spread across her face when she opens it Christmas morning."

"Are you all going to be at your parents' house this year, or at one of your siblings'?"

Emy places a piece of tape on one of the sides of wrapping paper. "My folks'. They're so excited; they can't wait to have the whole family together. We only get to see everyone all together during the holidays, so they really look forward to it. I'm just excited to see Skye and Lily. It's been so long since I got to spoil those two babies of mine."

Skye and Lily are her oldest brother's twins. They live out in California.

"Anyway, don't think I forgot. I still think we need to analyze your feelings for Guns right now."

Fuck, I thought I was safe. "Oh, no, we don't."

She smirks at me. "Oh, yes, we do. Don't make me call Shannon to stop by after work so we can torture you."

I frown. "Please don't."

She laughs. "Okay, fine. But we're going to be talking about this soon. If not now, tomorrow. You hear me?"

I nod.

"No. Do you hear me?" She places a hand behind her ear, acting like it will help her hear me.

I want to roll my eyes, but instead of prolonging the inevitable, I look up at the ceiling and say, "Yes, I hear you, Ms. Emerson."

A smile spreads on her face. "That's better. Now help me finish wrapping these last couple of gifts."

After leaving Emy's, I pull up to the convenience store a few blocks from my house to pick up some bacon, eggs, and pancake mix for tomorrow morning. Every Tuesday morning, Shannon stops by and we usually have breakfast together. We both have the day off.

Yeah, we see each other all the time, including the time we spend with Emy together. But breakfast on Tuesdays at my place has been an ongoing tradition for as long as I can remember. It's a sister-sister type thing. It's one thing I'm never going to give up.

I reach the front entrance of the store, and thankfully, they're still open. I've made it just in time with twenty minutes to spare. I need to be in and out. It shouldn't be a problem. It's a small store with only the bare necessities.

Making my way through the empty store, save for the manager behind the register, I pick up the items I need for tomorrow morning. I place the eggs, pancake mix, and bacon onto the counter and wait for the man to ring me up.

"Good evening, miss. Find everything you need all right?"

I smile at him, recognizing him from the other times I've been here. He's probably in his mid-sixties with salt-and-pepper hair. He's always very nice and well-mannered. Even though I come here quite often because it's close to my house, we never converse much besides small talk. "Yes, thank you."

"Twenty-three fifty-six," he responds.

I hand over two Jacksons and wait for my change. Once he gives it to me, I grab my groceries from the counter. "Thanks so much. Have a good night."

"You too, miss."

I walk out of the store and toward my car. It's a pretty quiet evening. A star-filled sky illuminates the area, and a shimmering crescent moon hangs overhead. A chilly breeze whooshes through the trees. It feels as though we're going to be hit with our first snowstorm of the year. I wouldn't mind it on Christmas Day, but any other time, it's a no from me. I'm not fond of the fluffy white stuff.

I finally reach my car and unlock it, and as I pull open the door, I almost drop the bag to the ground.

"It's so nice to see you again, Carissa babe."

A gasp escapes my throat as I spin around and am greeted by the last person on Earth I want to see right now.

"Steve… You scared me."

He smirks and walks closer to me. He looks trashed. Shit.

"My apologies, babe. I've been waiting almost ten minutes for you to come out of the store… I guess I'm just excited to see you again."

I furrow my brows, cocking my head to the side. "You've been watching me?"

He shakes his head and makes a tsking sound. "*Waiting*. I was waiting." He takes more steps forward, surprising me with his speedy movements, and pins me against the car. The groceries now fall to the ground. There go the eggs.

"Steve… the groceries. What are you doing?"

He brushes a finger underneath my chin and breathes heavily. His breath is warm and smells of booze. I knew it. He is trashed. He's definitely been drinking again.

"Oh, Carissa babe. I've been thinking about you and our little… *drama act*, shall we call it, the other night." His hands reach out to grab mine and places them on either side of my head.

He pushes up against me, and I feel his hard-on through his pants. Ugh. I don't want to be anywhere near him right now. I fight to lift my arms and push him away, but I can't. Even wasted, he's still stronger than me.

"Let me go, Steve. Please," I beg.

His grin turns upside down. His eyebrows narrow.

My heart races. I'm in trouble. "Please don't do this… Let me go," I beg again.

"No!" He quickly bangs my hands against the car.

"You're hurting me, Steve! Stop!" I scream, hoping the owner of the convenience store might hear me. Maybe he'll run out and see me and then call the cops. Fuck… I need to find a way to alert him or free myself.

"Shut up, bitch! You're gonna attract company!"

"That's the point!" I drive my knee into his groin, which finally makes him loosen his hold on me.

"Ow, you slut!" He bends in half, holding on to his sacred area.

I rush to get away, but before I know it, he grabs me again.

"Oh, no you don't. You're coming with me. Let's go," he commands.

"No!" I roar, fighting with all my might to get free from his hold once more.

A stern, masculine voice sounds from behind me. "Let her go."

I snap my head around and see Lorenzo's terrifying glare fixated on my ex.

Steve doesn't let go of me, but his hold has definitely loosened a bit. "Who the fuck are—wait, you look a lot like… No, you can't be… You're not—"

"Lorenzo Trevano, UFC Heavyweight Champion." Lorenzo steps closer and into the glow from the streetlight, and now I get a better glimpse of his face. Even as the rage pours out in his tone, he's still gorgeous.

Steve finally lets go of me, and I take a few steps to get farther away from him.

Lorenzo's hard gaze stares directly into Steve's eyes. "Now, I believe the lady wants to be left alone. I advise you to take a hike, or you can deal with me. The choice is yours."

Steve looks back at me, probably not believing the champion is standing right before us, defending me. I know from back when we were dating, he used to watch MMA all the time. I know he's got to be familiar with Lorenzo. He quickly averts his eyes back to Guns.. "You've got to be kidding me."

Lorenzo's gaze doesn't soften. "I assure you this isn't a joke. You either take your ass out of here *willingly*, or I'll take it out for you. It's totally up to you."

Steve grimaces. "Fuck this. You're not worth it, bitch," he spits at me.

Lorenzo chuckles. "Oh, hell no." It's crystal clear by his tone that he's not amused. Not one bit. He calmly walks up to Steve and grabs him by the collar of his shirt. "Apologize to Carissa, or you're going to be one *very* sorry piece of shit."

My eyes take in Steve's horrified expression as he visibly swallows hard. "O-okay, okay. I'm sorry!" he trembles.

Lorenzo chuckles again. "Not to me... *to her.*"

Steve sticks his head out to the side to be sure I can see him. "Carissa, I'm sorry... I'm sorry."

Lorenzo pulls Steve back and glares him down. Steve is a good four inches shorter and is definitely not as muscular. Lorenzo is towering over him, and the look on Steve's face is enough to make this evening worth my while. I would have paid a million bucks to see him look the way he does right now.

"Good, now get lost and don't let me catch you bothering Miss Carissa again. Scram!" Lorenzo shoves him away, and Steve runs off.

"Thank you so much," I say after Steve's out of sight as I bend down to pick up my groceries. The eggs are all cracked, but the bacon and pancake mix are fine. I'll just tell Shannon to pick up a carton on her way over tomorrow morning. No big deal.

He smiles at me, bending down as well, and hands me the box of pancake mix.

"No cream cheese this time?" He smiles.

I want to melt.

My breath catches in my throat. He's so fine... so gorgeous... *so off limits.* Like I said before, I know he's got to be a playboy. There's no way a man this fine—*and a gentleman at that*—doesn't have women lined up waiting to have an evening with him. I know I would be.

"Thanks," I say, taking the box of pancake mix from him.

"It's nothing, really. And that little episode? I'm glad I

found you when I did. That could have gone a lot worse." He takes a deep breath and then speaks again. "What are you doing out here all by yourself? It's getting late."

We rise to our feet and stand across from one another. I almost get lost in my thoughts, staring into his big brown eyes.

"I had some things I needed to grab for tomorrow morning. I shop here at this time often, but this is the first time something like this has happened to me."

"Let's hope it's the last."

I nod. "Definitely."

"Okay, I'll wait till you get into your car and drive off before I get going. Just to make sure," he states.

"Thanks." I walk to the driver's side of my car and hop in behind the wheel.

Lorenzo walks up to my car, so I lower the window.

"Drive carefully, Carissa."

I smile. "Thanks, I will."

"Hey, wait a second," he says. "Do you have a pen?"

"Sure," I fumble through the glove compartment and pull out a blue ink pen. "Here you are."

He grabs it from me, and our hands brush yet again, sending electricity flowing through me. Just one touch from him sends me zooming. It's just like the first time at the grocery store. It seems like we've got a thing going on with groceries.

I chuckle to myself as he pulls a small piece of paper from his back pocket and scribbles something on it. When he's done, he hands it to me with the pen. "That's my number. Call me if you ever need me again… or text me if you just want to talk."

I swallow thickly. Holy shit… his number? Emy and Shannon will have a field day with this.

"Thanks, I will."

He smiles again, tapping the frame of my window. "Cool. All right, I'll let you go now. Have a great night, Carissa."

I smile back. "Good night, Lorenzo."

He pushes away from the car. Reluctantly, I push the button to close the window and drive away into the night.

Chapter Twelve

LORENZO

What are the odds, running into the girl you can't get out of your mind again and finding she needs your help? What a douchebag that guy was. We didn't get to talk much, but from what I picked up from the conversation, they surely had a past. I can't imagine anyone treating her the way he was. I hope that when they were together, he treated her better than what I witnessed. Sure, he was drunk off his ass, but c'mon. I've been drunk before, and I would never dream of treating a woman the way he was treating her.

Thank God I had decided to go for a run at the last minute. I was supposed to hit the shower once I got home, but Gianna was still up and she didn't want Marianna to leave quite yet. So she stayed with her while I went jogging. It felt so good to run and not think of much. I blasted my music on my AirPods and let each thud of my step release the day's stress. It was all going so well until a woman across the street caught my attention from the corner of my eyes. Lo and behold, it was her. Two blocks from my house, I saw Carissa, and the rest was history.

Sure, it was a risky move giving her my number.

Honestly, I don't know what came over me, but it was on impulse. I hadn't taken two seconds to think about it, and it hadn't crossed my mind at all before she was about to pull away. It was as if one minute I'm bidding her adieu, and the next, I'm pulling out a piece of paper and scribbling my number across it.

The piece of paper? A receipt from the 7-Eleven near the gym. I had stopped by momentarily after my workout to grab a bottle of Cool Blue Gatorade.

I quietly tiptoe inside my house and see Marianna sitting on the couch, typing something on her phone.

"Hey, is she out?" I ask, closing the door behind me.

She puts her phone down and looks up at me. "Yeah, after ten minutes, she cuddled up against my side and fell asleep. I just put her down in her bed like five minutes ago." She stands and stretches her arms.

"Thanks."

She shakes her head. "It's nothing. I love watching her. You know that." She pauses for a moment and then says, "I was starting to get worried about you…"

I furrow my brows. I guess I was gone longer than I had told her I was going to be. "I'm sorry." I don't really want to get into it with her. If she knew I got into an altercation with some drunk guy over a random girl, she wouldn't be too happy with me.

But is Carissa just some random girl? We're friends now, aren't we?

She raises an eyebrow and smirks. "I hope you didn't get into any trouble."

Now I have to look away. The only thing I need is for her to find out my taking longer than expected had something to do with some girl. I pretend to busy myself with tidying up, grabbing magazines and crayons off the living room coffee table. She and Gianna must have been coloring in her princess and pony coloring books.

"Lorenzo?"

"Hmm?" I lift my head in her direction, but I continue looking at the table in front of me.

She grabs my arm. "You're not telling me something."

I finally lift my gaze to meet hers and shrug. "I may have had to help a friend of mine." I pull away and pretend like it's no big deal.

Marianna throws up her arms in exasperation. "Lorenzo! You know you have a temper that can get you into loads of trouble! I don't want to see the cops arresting you because you can't control your emotions. You have a little girl you need to put first, before some muscle head friend of yours from the gym!"

My sister loves to throw that little incident from three years ago in my face whenever she can. I got into a fight with a neighbor that caused the people upstairs to call the cops, and yeah... I was brought into the station. It wasn't my fault, but I may have had a little bit too much to drink, thinking about my miserable life, and there went that.

But that all happened three years ago, and there hasn't been another incident since. I've been on my best behavior. I need to be anyway, for my little girl. It's just that sometimes, my temper gets the best of me. It is why I turned to mixed martial arts. I get to let my anger loose and not get in trouble with the law.

In a matter of milliseconds, my anger rises, and I explode. "It wasn't a guy from the gym! Carissa was being harassed by her asshole ex-boyfriend. I needed to intervene. He was getting physical with her..." I blurt. Crap, I couldn't control my mouth. The last thing I wanted to do was tell her about Carissa.

Her shocked expression is exactly what I expect. She folds her arms across her chest. "*Carissa*? Who's this Carissa you so casually speak of?"

I shrug. Might as well face the music now rather than

later. "The chick Max was teasing me about since the night we went to the bar. I saw her again at the supermarket the other day, and just now when I went jogging. She needed help. I couldn't just turn a blind eye and let the guy have his way with her."

She nods. "Of course not. You did the right thing. I just hope the cops weren't involved."

"No, he ran off with his tail between his legs."

She chuckles. "Good. I would think so. I mean, look at you."

I cock my head.

"You're a beast, Enz. Anyone ballsy enough to stand up to you is crazy." She takes a few steps forward, heading toward the door.

"Hey, Mari?"

She turns around. "Yeah, Enz?"

"Don't mention this to Max, okay?"

Smiling, she says, "Of course not. He would never let you live it down. I'm glad I have a brother who is such a wonderful man. She's lucky to have you."

"Wait, I'm not *with* her *with her*... you know. She's not... We're not—"

"Lorenz, I know," she says, cutting me off. "I'm saying she's lucky to have you as a friend. Nothing more." She winks at me, and it makes me feel like she's hoping there soon will be something more between us. Great.

After Marianna goes home, I quickly peek into Gianna's room to check on her. She's sound asleep with the sweetest smile on her face. My pretty little princess. She melts my heart.

I leave the door cracked open and hit the shower. Once I

finish, I get myself ready for bed. I slide in between the sheets, but I'm restless. Too much is on my mind, and I can't fall asleep.

Okay, I lied. Not too much. But maybe too much of someone.

I grab my cell phone off the nightstand and scroll through my Instagram feed. Pictures of my friends' days and celebrity posts fill my screen. After liking a few, I check Facebook. I do the same: like a few posts, comment on some, and turn it off.

As I place my cell phone back onto my nightstand, it vibrates, alerting me of a new message. I lift it again and bring it back to me.

Hi, it's Carissa.

With those three words, my heart stops. I store her number in my contacts and compose a text back.

Me: Hi, Carissa. How are you? Get home okay?

So maybe it wasn't the best opener, and it may sound like she's disturbing me, like: *"Good you got home okay. I'm assuming because you're texting me. Now can you please fuck off?"*

Fuck. That's not how I wanted it to sound. I'm so thrilled she texted me already. I honestly didn't think I'd be hearing from her, especially not now. But me texting her if she's okay makes it seem like I want her to say what she has to say and get on with it. Dammit.

Carissa: Yes, thank you. I got home just fine. But I wanted to thank you again for rescuing me tonight ;) It was very sweet of you.

A smile spreads on my face from ear to ear. I'm glad she

texted me back. Now I can think of something better to say and possibly talk to her for a little while.

> **Me: Hey, it's no problem. I'm just glad I was able to be there when you needed me.**

> **Me: So what are you up to? I'm just lying here in bed and can't fall asleep :/**

I hit send, but two minutes later, there's still no reply. Maybe she doesn't want to talk to me after all. Maybe she was just being polite and thanking me once more before going to sleep.

I kick myself. *You blew it, Lorenzo. Way to go.*

I exit out of the text messaging app and refresh my Facebook and Instagram feeds and then my phone alerts me again. My heartbeat speeds up.

It's another message, but once I realize it's not from Carissa, I frown. I open it anyway.

> **Ryker: Lorenz, you up?**

> **Me: Yeah, what's up, bro?**

We spend the next couple of minutes texting back and forth about the upcoming Christmas party at the gym. I frown when twenty minutes later there's still no reply from Carissa.

"So I'm thinking of bringing Justine. What do you think?" Ryker asks as we're in the locker room getting ready to start warm-ups.

I throw my boots into the locker and fumble through to find my gloves. They're somewhere in here, but ever since last night, I haven't been able to function. I fell asleep sometime around 1:00 a.m., but the first thing I did when I awoke this morning at seven was check my phone. Still no text back from Carissa. She must really think she made a mistake by texting me in the first place. I should have just said you're welcome and called it a night. Why did I try to start a conversation with a woman who probably is turned off by men, thanks to her wonderful ex or whoever he was to her?

I mean, I'm not trying to start seeing women right now, but I wouldn't mind getting to know her, considering we keep running into one another and I helped her last night.

I'm nowhere near ready to start dating. No matter what my family or my friends say, Sylvia will always be my wife, and I can't bring myself to find someone new. It wouldn't be fair to her. The thought makes me sad.

"Earth to Lorenzo. Come in, Lorenzo... You alive, bro?" Ryker waves a hand in my direction, catching my attention.

"What? Oh, I'm sorry, dude. You said something about your baby mama?"

He chuckles. "Yeah, I wanted to bring Justine to the party, but yo, where's your head at? I've been trying to talk to you all morning, and you've been totally spacing. What's going on with you?"

I slam my locker shut and lean against it, adjusting the straps on my gloves. "Just got some stuff on my mind, nothing serious. But yeah, I think that's great about Justine. You guys getting along again?"

"We are, and I've been seeing her and Mandy every night after work. I think we're really hitting it off again."

I smile. "That's great, man. I'm happy for you."

He closes his locker. "Thanks, bro. But now, what's up with you? You know you can talk to me, right?"

I'm about to dismiss him again and not get into it, but what the hell? He's the one who always tells me I need to make some more friends, and why not females? I don't necessarily have to tell him I've been thinking about Carissa as much as I have been, but I can tell him I misread her texts.

That was for sure. I was certain she wanted to start a conversation with me last night over it, but instead, it seems she was just being polite.

"It's not a big deal, but there's this girl who—"

"Oh, hell yeah. Go for it," he says, cutting me off.

I chuckle. "Man, you don't even know what I was going to say."

He places a foot on the bench and ties his laces. "Doesn't matter. You mentioned a girl, and, dude, you need to get laid."

I feel my anger starting to rise. I'm not trying to get laid. For fuck's sake, why is it always about that? Can't a man and a woman be friends without sex being involved?

I want to ask him, but I know it won't get me anywhere. I compose myself so this doesn't turn into another MMA match. "It's not about *getting laid*, man."

"It's always about getting laid. But continue."

I swallow hard and try to push aside what I really want to say to him right now. "Anyway, there's this girl I'm constantly running into everywhere."

I go on to tell him about how I first saw her at the bar with her friends, then at the match, followed by our supermarket cream cheese episode and then my encounter with her asshole ex-boyfriend. I finally tell him about our text conversation, and he just listens to every word and all my concerns.

"Damn, Enz. That's crazy."

Some of the guys exit the locker room and make their way to the floor. We should be joining them right about now, but I need to talk. I didn't realize how badly I needed this until Ryker pushed me to do it.

"Yeah, so I was going to try to make a friend, but you see where it got me. I need to just realize it's not for me. My love came and went. It's just me and my princess and—"

The sound of my phone going off stops me mid-sentence.

Ryker chuckles. "Dude, if that's her, she wants you. No doubt about it. If she didn't, she wouldn't have texted you back anymore."

I avert my gaze from him without saying a word. I unlock my locker and ravage through my things to find my cell phone in my bag. It could be Gianna's school, but if it was the school, wouldn't they call instead? My ringtone is different from my notification tone. And as a matter of fact, each notification sound is different. This one was definitely a text message, but it could be anyone.

A new text message from Carissa is waiting for me.

I look back at Ryker, who is standing over my shoulder trying to see if it is indeed her.

"It's her... Carissa."

Ryker jumps. "I told you, bro! She wants you! Invite her to Friday's party!"

I turn around with the phone still in my hand. "Are you crazy, Ryke?"

"Why am I crazy?"

I smirk. "I haven't even checked what her message says. For all I know, she could be asking me not to text her anymore, and you're telling me to invite her to our company's Christmas party? No way, dude."

He steps back with a look on his face that tells me he's not satisfied with my reply. "It's just a party... not like a romantic dinner date. You could get to know her with a ton of people around so neither one of you feels uncomfortable. Maybe she doesn't want to date right now after what you told me happened to her in the parking lot, but Enz, I'm telling you. If she's texting you back now after so many hours of being silent, she definitely likes you. Trust me."

I think about his words for a second but don't say anything. If the party wasn't going to be offering alcohol, kids would be welcomed, and I could bring Gianna. But since I can't bring her, he does make a valid point. The party would be the perfect way to get to know her without technically asking her out on a date.

"Bro, check your text. See what she said," Ryker says, reminding me why I have the phone in my hand in the first place.

I nod and open the message from her.

> **Carissa: Hey! I'm so sorry I didn't respond back last night... I passed out and woke up with my phone in my hand. So to answer your question, I was lying in bed myself, not able to fall asleep. :)**

Immediately after reading her message, thoughts of her lying in a bed cross my mind. What the fuck? What is wrong with me? I shake my head to get the thought of her out of my mind.

"She passed out while we were talking. That's why she never responded back," I say to Ryker, who nods his head.

"Good, now ask her."

"What?"

He comes forward, motioning for me to message her back. "Let her know about the party. Ask her to come."

I swallow hard. Do I have the balls to ask this woman to the company party? What are people going to think? Fuck, man. Why is this so difficult?

"I can't do it."

Ryker chuckles. "Why the fuck not, dude? It's just a party."

"What are people going to think? That she's my girlfriend?"

"Who cares what the fuck people think! It's none of their goddamn business if she were your girlfriend. But she's just a friend, and you can introduce her as that, or fuck it, don't introduce her to anyone you don't want to. It's none of their damn business what you do with your life anyway."

He has a point. Who cares what people think? And if I really wanted to date five years after my wife passed away, would that be so wrong?

Yes, to me, it would be. But I'm not dating Carissa, and I have the right to have a female friend if I want one. Everyone can go suck a nut.

"Okay, here goes nothing," I say, hitting the box in the app to type my response.

> **Me: Hey, it's no problem. Happens to me all the time. Listen, if you're not busy this Friday night—**

"No, dude! Don't give her the option to chicken out and say she's busy. Tell her you want her to go with you. Be bold," Ryker states, hovering over my shoulder once more.

I move away a bit. "Dude, okay... okay. Jeez."

I delete the last part of the message and rephrase it.

> **Me: Hey, it's no problem. Happens to me all the time. The company I work for is having a holiday party this Friday... I'd love it if you would come and check it out.**

"Much better," Ryker says after I hit the send button.

I chuckle and shake my head. "I'm glad you approve."

"No problem, bro."

My phone goes off again a few seconds later.

Carissa: I would love to join you.

"She said yes," I tell him in shock.

A huge smile spreads across his face, illuminating the entire locker room. "I fuckin' told you, bro. She wants you."

I roll my eyes, put my phone away, and we make our way into the practice area of the gym.

Chapter Thirteen

CARISSA

"I think I should fake a headache or pretend I'm hugging the toilet from food poisoning. I should cancel," I say, staring at my reflection in the mirror.

I'm wearing a black miniskirt and a red top with heels to match. Shannon and Emy spent the last two hours doing my hair and makeup.

"Cariss, would you like to get slapped now or later?" Shannon asks, standing behind me.

I flip around with a frown, diverting my gaze from Shannon to Emy. "What if this is a big mistake?"

"Carissa, would you stop second-guessing yourself? It's just a party. He didn't ask you to sleep with him, but ooh, if he did," Emy says, and they both laugh.

"I'm serious, guys. I'm really nervous." I look at the ground before Shannon places a finger underneath my chin.

"Hey, sis. If I thought this was a bad idea, I'd tell you. But I think it's great. You keep running into the UFC heavyweight champion, and he's a damn hot piece of man candy… like, seriously. You'll be fine."

"Shannon's right, girl. The boy is fiiiine!"

Now the three of us are laughing.

I was a little hesitant when I texted him the other night after the incident with Steve; I'll admit that. But when I awoke the next morning and saw another text sitting there in my inbox from him, something inside me said to go for it.

"Okay, I guess it's okay," I say and turn around to get one last glimpse in the mirror.

"Is he picking you up?" Emy asks.

"I'm meeting him there. He offered, but I didn't want it to really feel like a date. He didn't seem upset about it at all."

They nod, and Shannon goes to sit on my bed while Emy pops a piece of gum into her mouth.

"Well, girl. Then you'd better get going 'cause you're going to be late," Shannon states.

I look over at the time and notice it is indeed time to go.

T he girls and I walk out of my building and then they walk me to my car to make sure I don't chicken out. I keep telling them they don't have to, but they insist.

They wait to make sure I pull out of the parking spot, but as I go to start the car, nothing is happening.

"She's backing out," I hear Emerson say from right outside my car.

Shannon moves closer to it and places her hands on the ledge of the window. "What's going on?"

I meet her gaze. "I don't know. I can't get it to start."

"Let me see."

I hop out and she hops in. She tries to bring the engine to life, but nothing is happening.

"Of course this shit happens to me. Maybe this is a sign from God, low key telling me it's not meant to be," I say, pacing back and forth.

Emy leans against the piece of shit that won't start. "Oh,

no. Don't you do that. Call him and see if he can come pick you up."

I look at her like she's got three heads. "Woman, are you crazy?"

"No, Carissa. She's serious. Now, call or text Lorenzo—I don't care which—and have him come grab you," Shannon says.

For a second, I don't move. The last thing I want to do is call him right now, but they're not giving me any other option.

"Can't one of you two just give me a ride? It's not that—"

"Call him!" the two of them say in unison.

I let out a deep breath and plop my ass against my car. Damn piece of tin that won't start, I hate you so much right now.

I pull out my cell phone from my purse and call Lorenzo.

"I'm glad you didn't stand me up. I don't think my ego could take that," Lorenzo says with a smile once he pulls into the parking lot.

I chuckle. "I was so close. You have my best friend and sister to thank."

He looks gorgeous. The fact that he's smiling right now only makes it better. He's wearing a gray dress shirt over black pants. I think Emy and Shannon almost passed out when they saw him pull up. When he stepped out of the car... forget it.

"Are you very close to them?" he asks.

"Yes, they're my ride-or-dies," I respond, fussing with some strands of hair.

He pulls into a spot and kills the engine. "That's cool. I have a best friend named Ryker who I'm tight with. You'll meet him tonight. And then of course, there's my sister and brother who I'm also very close to."

I nod. "Is it the same Ryker from the tournament?"

His smile widens. "Yes, that's the one. I'm surprised you remember him."

"Emy wouldn't let me forget if I tried."

He chuckles. "Okay, we're here. This is where we hold our practices and some of our smaller tournaments. But don't worry, it doesn't smell like sweaty gym socks. We cleaned up and decorated the place for the party."

I giggle. "I'm not at all worried. Trust me, I don't work in the most *elegant* environment all the time either."

"Oh, yeah? What do you do?"

I shrug. "I work at the hospital. It's not very pleasant sometimes."

His smile fades, and I instantly wonder what I said wrong. Of all the things we've talked about over the last couple of days through text message, my job never came up. We discussed so much, including our favorite types of food, music, and movies, but what I did for a living happened to slip both of our minds.

"All right, let's get going. Are you ready?" he asks.

I take a deep breath and respond. "I'm ready."

We step out of the car and walk up to the main entrance.

"Lorenzo's Fitness Center… you own this?"

He smiles. "I do."

Holy shit. I didn't know he was the owner.

He opens the door for me, and when we step foot inside, I see the whole gym is decorated in red and green embellishments. Colorful lights bounce off the walls, reminding me of school dances I attended as a kid growing up. Glittered snowmen and snowflakes line the wall, music fills the air, and a table full of holiday treats is set up against the wall.

"You guys decorated all of this?" I ask, my eyes in awe of the beauty.

He places a hand on the small of my back, causing that same bolt of electricity I felt the other night come rushing back through me.

"We sure did. I couldn't have a party here if it looked like crap. Let's get our coats checked and then head on inside."

He leads me inside the center area of the gym, and almost instantly, Ryker walks up to us.

"Hey, Enz! You made it, bro!" he shouts. He's holding a drink in one hand. Behind him, a woman with red hair wearing a dress that resembles a piece of lingerie comes forward.

"Hey, Ryker," Lorenzo says, embracing his friend. "This is Carissa Rodgers. Carissa, this is my best friend and the biggest goofball you'll ever meet, Ryker Manzoni."

"Hi, Ryker," I say.

"Carissa, it's lovely to meet you. This is my girlfriend, Justine." He gently pushes her forward.

Her cold, surly smile sends chills up my back. Shit. Winter doesn't have anything on her cold and stuck-up personality.

I smile politely, and thankfully, Lorenzo saves me. "Justine, it's so good to see you again. How's Mandy?"

Her chilling smile fades, and her green eyes dart toward Lorenzo. "*Amanda?* She's well, thank you."

"So, have you checked out the bar? It's nice..." Ryker states and drains the rest of his drink.

Lorenzo chuckles. "For what they charged? It better be."

Holy crap... I can only imagine how much this is costing him, more so because he invited me. I would have felt like a bitch if I had made up some excuse not to come. Thank God for my two girls, pushing me to attend tonight.

"Yeah, well, there's a shit ton of catered food coming in just a bit, and the music, the DJ... the drinks of course. I wanted the best for tonight," Lorenzo states.

"It must have cost an arm and a leg. Everything is so much money," Ryker responds.

"As it should," Justine abruptly responds.

No one says a word, but the look on Ryker's face says he's not all too thrilled. I wonder if she's always like this when she's with him or if she just doesn't want to be here. From what I've witnessed so far, Ryker seems to be a really nice guy, but like I said, so far. I don't really know him. Lorenzo has spoken highly of him every single time he's talked about him.

"Well, let's go grab a drink," Ryker says as he throws his empty cup in the garbage to our left and grabs Justine's hand.

Lorenzo and I exchange a look, and I swear I can feel my panties melting. He is incredibly hot, and whenever he smiles at me, I want to die. I don't remember the last time I've felt like this about anyone.

I want to melt into his gaze, and the sudden urge to get him in a corner and make out with him takes over me.

No idea where that's coming from, but fuck. He's gorgeous.

Breaking the spell, he turns to look at Ryker. "Dude, you already had a drink."

Ryker nods. "And now, it's time for another. Come on!"

"Did you enjoy yourself tonight?" Lorenzo asks as we buckle up. We said good-night to Ryker, Justine, and a few other guys he introduced me to from his gym, and now he's taking me home.

I smile and adjust myself in the seat. "It was so much fun. I don't go out too often, so this was really nice. The food and the music were great. Your friends and the staff all seem very nice too."

He chuckles, and the sound of it sends me swooning. Damn.

"Yeah, those guys are great, and Ryker is the best. Justine... not so much."

I place a hand over my mouth to stifle a laugh. "What's her deal anyway?"

He shrugs, pulling out of the parking lot. "She's his baby mama. They dated a while back, she got pregnant, and ever since Mandy came, she wasn't all that nice to him. She broke up with him and then she wouldn't allow him to see the baby for so long. She always hounded him for money, even though he always sent her more than what the government said he should. Plus, he always buys her anything and everything on top of it."

I furrow my brows. "I don't understand. If he's doing what he's supposed to and being a good dad, why is she acting like that toward him?"

He shrugs again. "I don't really know. I think she just likes drama."

We both chuckle before he continues.

"Nah, but now they are back together, so he's able to see his daughter again and be in her life like he wants without the drama. That little girl is everything to him."

I smile as we turn onto my block. "Aww, how old is she?"

"She just turned four." He pauses for a moment and then asks, "Do you have any kids?"

I shake my head, even though he can't take his eyes off the road and look at me right now. "No. Do you?"

He doesn't answer for a moment, and it seems as though he carefully chooses his next words. "I do. Gianna. She's five."

I nod. I'm not surprised he does. I kind of expected it. He is gorgeous. Of course he had tons of women before me, and of course he was with someone long enough to have a baby with them. I wonder if he gets along with her. I hope for his daughter's sake they do get along, but I secretly hate the thought that there was someone else before me.

Before me. Listen to me, thinking there's even a chance for us. I don't want one. I want to stay single. Don't I?

"So, no kids... What about overprotective husbands?" He smiles, and I'm once again falling all over myself.

"No... I was engaged at one point, but it didn't go anywhere."

He pulls into a spot in front of my building. "Was it with the guy from the other night?"

I smile nervously. "Steve. Yeah... that was him."

He turns to face me, and I want to melt into a puddle. Holy crap, the weight of his stare is causing so many emotions to flow through me right now. As against as I was about dating again after Steve, I want Lorenzo right now. I want him to kiss me with those full lips of his. I want him to place his huge hands on me and take me to where I haven't been in so long.

"His loss," he whispers, and I surely wasn't expecting that.

God, this stare of his is making me drench my panties all over again.

"We're here," I say, trying desperately to divert this conversation because I really don't think I'm ready for it.

He leans in closer and chuckles softly. My heart races. It seems like he wants to kiss me. Lord, do I want him to. Even if I am scared and changed the subject just moments ago.

Instead of kissing me like I'm hoping, he speaks again. "We are, but I'd really like to see you again, Carissa."

Holy shit... he would? Damn, so would I. Honestly, I don't even want this night to end now. Do I invite him in?

I swallow thickly. "I'd like that very much."

His smile is still spread across his handsome face. My heart pounds in my chest, and my palms grow sweaty.

"Good. I'll text you. Let me walk you to your door."

"Okay," I respond breathlessly.

He walks around to my side of the car and opens the door for me before I have a chance to get out. He helps me out, and I grab his hand. I swear, the lightning bolts of electricity I felt earlier and the other night are back once more. This guy is going to be the death of me.

We stop when we reach the entrance to my building, and I'm left standing inches away from him, looking up into his gorgeous brown eyes.

He looks away for only a split second before coming back to my gaze. "I'm really glad you came with me to the party tonight. I really enjoyed your company."

"I did too."

He leans in a few inches, hesitates for a moment, and pulls back. "Good night, Carissa."

Damn, I thought this was surely the moment he was going to kiss me.

"Good night, Lorenzo," I respond and then he turns around and walks to his car.

I wave before entering the building, and after I close the door and watch from the window above it, he disappears into the dark of night.

Chapter Fourteen

LORENZO

I run a hand through Gianna's hair and watch Ryker take another bite of his pepperoni slice. His daughter, Mandy, is sitting to his left, drinking some juice.

It's been two days since the party, and we decided to bring the girls out for some pizza and games. Two dads and their little girls... What could be better?

"So, how's it been being back home?" I ask.

Ryker lifts his gaze after scarfing down yet another bite.

I shake my head. "Dude, I don't know how you can eat that stuff like it's actually good. My brother is the same way."

"It is good," he says through a mouthful. "It's great." He swallows, takes a gulp of his drink, and wipes his mouth. "Chuck E. Cheese pizza is the best. I knew I liked your brother for some reason."

"Daddy, can we go play now?" Mandy asks Ryker, pulling on his sleeve.

Ryker turns to face her, but I have to intervene.

"As soon as your daddy is done with his eleventh slice, we'll go play, sweetheart."

Mandy frowns at me. "He's taking too long."

"I know, right?" I whisper back.

Ryker throws me a glare. "Thanks a lot, bro."

I snicker. "No problem."

"Daddy, Uncle Ryke eats so much like Uncle Maxy." Gianna now is tugging on my sleeve, grabbing my attention.

Ryker throws me another glare.

I face my little girl and place a kiss on her forehead. I want to laugh at her statement. "He does. See, when you're a big muscle head, like your Uncle Ryke there, you need to eat a lot of not-so-good food."

"But I like Chuck E. Cheese pizza! It is good!" Gianna exclaims. Her big blue eyes shine like diamonds. Damn, she looks so much like her mother.

I frown.

"I'm sorry, Daddy. I know it's not very good for you." Gianna throws her little arms as best as she can around me. She doesn't even make it halfway around.

"Oh, no, princess. I'm not upset with you. It's okay to like this pizza. Daddy is only joking. Uncle Ryke and Uncle Maxy like it too." I grab her into my arms and set her in my lap. Then, looking at both girls, I say, "Come on. I think Uncle Ryke is done eating. Let's go play."

"Yay!" they shout in unison.

We slide out of the seats and head to the arcade games. The girls run to similar ones next to each other, and Ryker and I swipe our key cards so they can play.

While they're playing, we stand behind them and watch them have a ball.

I cross my arms across my chest and decide to ask him again about things with Justine. He didn't really answer me the first time.

I want the best for my best friend, but I'm not so sure Justine is it for him. I know she's the mother of his child and he loves her, but I don't think she cares about him as much as he does her. It's a shame though. They could be a nice little family, but instead, she usually acts like a bitch.

"How's things going since you moved back, dude?"

Ryker looks at me and smiles widely. "I've been getting laid every night."

I shake my head. "That's not what I asked you."

Ryker shrugs, chuckling. "You know Justine, man. One minute she's wonderful, affectionate and loving. The next, she doesn't want to be bothered. I'm just happy to be seeing Mandy every single day."

I nod. "I know you are, bro. But I hate that she's like night and day with you, and you never know how she's going to react to something. Is this how you really want to spend the rest of your life?"

He shrugs again, and this time his smile is gone. "I don't know. What am I supposed to do, man? Leave and only see Mandy when it suits her?"

I wave my hands in front of me. "Not at all. That's not what I'm saying. But are you only with her to see Mandy?"

"Daddy! Mandy and I want to go in the ball pit! Can we? Can we? Please!" Gianna tugs on the side of my jeans.

I look down at her and nod. "Of course, princess. Let's head over there."

The four of us walk to the ball pit and maze of plastic tubes. Kids running around like monkeys and their parents chasing after them surround us. The girls flick their shoes off and dart to the ball pit while Ryker and I place them in adjacent cubbies.

We make sure to have a good view of the girls and take a seat on one of the nearby benches.

"I don't know, Enz. I love Justine. Don't get me wrong. But I'm not so sure she always loves me, you know?" Ryker finally says more than asks.

I lean forward and place my elbows on my knees. "I totally understand, and I sort of sensed it. That's why I asked. It's a difficult situation, but you definitely shouldn't be with someone if you don't feel they love you as much as you love them."

"What about Mandy? I love seeing my little girl every day. The thought of being away from her again for days and sometimes weeks at a time kills me." He stares at her as she plays with Gianna in the ball pit, and I know it would really tear him up inside to be away from her again.

I frown. I know where he's coming from because I would hate not to see my baby every single day. I've never been through what he has, but I know for a fact I would be devastated. Nothing means more to me than my princess.

"I know, Ryke. It's not something easy to go through. I'm praying things get better and she'll change and realize what she has."

"I hope so too, bro. Thanks."

I straighten and look at him. "For what?"

He shrugs. "For always having my back. For always looking out for me. For being the brother I never had."

I place an arm on his shoulder. "Of course, man. We're bros for life. You know I got you and your little girl, no matter what."

I could be mistaken, but he looks like he's getting a little teary-eyed.

"Thanks, Lorenzo."

I nod and sit back, letting my arm fall to the side.

Then he takes me by surprise. "So... How about Carissa?"

The mention of her name sends shivers up and down my spine. Fuck, she was something else. The way she looked Friday night... I could stare at her all evening.

Those lips of hers fucking called out to me so many times. I wanted to taste them so badly. Lord knows how many times they've crossed my mind, as well as all they can do.

Fuck. I need to get these thoughts off my brain. This isn't the damn time nor place for it.

But fuck, I was so close to kissing her. Both times I

tried, I chickened out. I couldn't do it. I was afraid and nervous. What if she'd pull away? What if she didn't want me to?

I was also very skeptical about bringing Gianna up in the conversation. My baby girl is my number one priority, but how would she feel about it? If I would have sensed she had a problem with me being a dad, I would have been gone. If someone can't accept my baby girl, then I know for sure they're not the one for me. We come as a package deal.

And Sylvia... I was about to tell Carissa about her, but I couldn't bring myself to get into it. Maybe another day, but Friday wasn't it.

I know if there is any chance of this going anywhere, I will need to tell her about Sylvia. For now, I want to keep things light and easy.

Damn, holding back from kissing her had not been easy at all. I was so close to leaning in and stealing a kiss from those succulent lips of hers... luscious lips...

Then Sylvia's face came to the front of my mind, so I left without looking back. Lord knows I had wanted to stay and kiss her, but I couldn't handle the guilt.

And yet, since I've met her, all I can think about is her. Even more so now since Friday. I think I'm falling for her.

Does that make me a bad guy? Does it mean I'm forgetting about Sylvia?

I frown and look at Ryker, not knowing what to say.

"What? What's the matter, bro? She ducking you?"

I shake my head. "No. Not at all. As a matter of fact, we've been nonstop talking and texting since that night. I can't get her out of my mind."

He smiles. "That's awesome, man. So why do you look like something is wrong?"

I shrug, take a deep breath, and look at my daughter, the spitting image of her mother. "How can I even begin to entertain the thought of being with another woman, bro? I look at Gianna, and all I see is Sylvs. How can I ever go down that route again?"

Ryker waves at the girls who just shouted excitedly to grab our attention. "Sure, Gianna does look like Sylvia a lot, but don't forget she's got a lot of you too. Look at her," he says, pointing at my daughter. "That's your smile right there."

It's true. I've heard so many times that my baby girl has my smile. I see it too. But the rest is all her mother. Okay, and maybe she has my strong-willed character too.

"I know," I say, not adding any more.

"Enz, you've gotta think of it this way. Sylvia would never have wanted you or Gianna to be sad or suffer. She wouldn't want to think it's because of her that you're holding back. It's been five years, dude. I think it's okay if you start dating again. Hell, it's even okay if you fall in love again. It doesn't mean you stopped loving your wife. Sylvia will always have a special place in your heart."

For the first time since meeting Ryker, he's speaking words with so much depth.

"Just think about it, bro. You don't have to marry her," he says.

He's right. Holding myself back isn't working. Carissa is on my mind all the time. When I'm not with her, we're talking through text or on the phone. She's not texting me now because she knows I'm out with Ryker. I told her it would be all right, but she insisted for me to just text her when I get back. She wanted me to enjoy time with my friend and our kids.

"You're right, bro," I say.

"Oh, I love hearing that. Tell me again."

I chuckle and hit Ryker in the arm. "Shut up, ass."

"I would say go get some right now, but I think I'll lay off the jokes for a while."

"Thanks, bro."

"Anytime, Enz. Anytime."

I put Gianna to bed and plop down onto the couch, pulling out my phone. I go into the text messaging app and bring up my conversation with Carissa.

I look at her picture on top and bite down on my bottom lip. She's beautiful. I still can't get over what a dumbass her ex was.

> *Me: Hey, beautiful. I just put Gianna to bed. We*
> *got home a little while ago. How was*
> *your day?*

I hit send before I even realize I called her beautiful. I don't think I should have said it, but hopefully she doesn't take it the wrong way.

I turn on the TV and flip through some channels. Nothing remotely entertaining catches my eye, but I only like silence when I'm lying in bed. Moments later, her reply comes through.

> *Carissa: Hey! Did you guys have fun? I'm about*
> *to drive home... I had to work last minute. My*
> *friend asked if I could fill in for her. It's been*
> *a long day. I can't wait to go home and lie*
> *in bed.*

Mmm. I would love to see that.

> *Me: Yeah, we had a great time. The girls had so*
> *much fun. I'm sorry you had a long day :(*
> *Grab a glass of wine when you get home.*

> *Carissa: LOL I don't drink much. But a glass of*

wine while lying in the bathtub does sound
like a dream. I love bubble baths.

Oh my God... bathtub? Jesus, I need to take this conversation into safer grounds. Now.

Me: Can I see you tomorrow?

Gianna is on break from school and is going to be spending the next couple of days at my parents' house. This will give me time to myself to do whatever I want. I love spending every minute with my daughter—don't get me wrong—but sometimes it's nice to only have to worry about myself. I know it sounds selfish, but that's the last thing I am. I just want to be selfish right now and see where this leads with Carissa. I'm not sure I can take it leading anywhere, but I'd like to take it step by step and see how I feel when I'm with her. Hanging out with her is going to be the only sure way for me to know if there can be anything between us at all. If she's off work tomorrow night, maybe she'll agree to seeing me again.

I wait for her to answer, but I'm growing impatient. Maybe it's too soon to see her again. Maybe she doesn't want to. Maybe I shouldn't have sent the last message, like I probably shouldn't have called her beautiful. She didn't seem to mind me calling her beautiful, I don't think. Well, at least I didn't type out Luscious Lips. How would I have explained that one to her without her hating me?

Damn, Lorenzo, get your shit together and don't fuck up.

I scroll up to reread the message she sent after I called her beautiful, but she seemed okay. Dammit, it's so hard to interpret how things are said when it's over text messages. Sometimes I wish people still talked on the phone like they used to instead of texting.

Twenty minutes pass before she texts me again.

> *Carissa: Just got home...for nine o'clock at night,
> there was more traffic than usual. But yes, I
> would love to see you tomorrow :)*

Phew, that's a relief.

> *Me: Perfect. Can I cook for you?*

> *Carissa: You cook?*

> *Me: I'm a single dad. I sure do.*

The realization of my text hits me hard. *Single dad.* I've never referred to myself as one before, even if I am, but talking to Carissa has made me say and type things I would have never imagined just weeks ago.

> *Carissa: I'm totally impressed. A hot guy who
> cooks? I'm sold :)*

A Kool-Aid Man smile forms on my face. She called me hot. Of course I know what most women think about me. I'm not stupid. Owning a gym, being a UFC fighter, and being in many tournaments, there are a ton of women around. I've always chosen to keep my distance because of Sylvia, but I've heard things and have had women throw their panties at me during matches. Carissa has been the first woman from the crowd I've tried to pursue.

> *Me: For you, I'd cook anything.*

What the hell was that? Quickly trying to redeem myself, I compose another text.

> *Me: Your ex didn't cook?*

Carissa: Steve? LOL no way. I had to wait on him hand and foot. He did nothing.

Me: :(that's crazy. I'm sorry.

Carissa: It's okay. It's not important now. What are you going to make for me?

Mmm, a nice dessert and load you up with whip cream...

Okay, what? My mind is in the gutter, but I'm choosing to blame her and her bubble bath images she forced me to think of.

Okay, maybe she didn't force me, but come on. The mention of it coming from her? How could I not?

Me: Do you like Italian?

Carissa: I LOVE Italian.

Nice. Then she'll adore me.

Jesus with the cheesiness. I need to cool off. I better hit the shower.

I decide to send her one last text for the night, because at this point, I'm going to be having a date with my hand within the next five minutes.

Me: Cool. I'll send you my address.

I type it to her, wish her a good-night, and hop off the couch.

This woman is going to be trouble for me... I can feel it.

Chapter Fifteen

LORENZO

"Is Auntie Mari going to get here soon? I want to go to Nonna's," Gianna whines, sitting patiently—or rather impatiently—for my sister to pick her up. She's twirling her hair around her finger.

The smell of dinner brewing in the oven fills the house. I'm hungry and can't wait to eat.

Marianna is running thirty minutes late. She got held up at work. I offered to drop Gianna off at my mother's house, but she insisted on waiting for her Auntie Mari. Apparently, she likes riding in her car better. Guess Daddy's truck is just not as cool as Auntie Mari's Audi.

It's Monday, four days before Christmas. Gianna is off from school for the next two weeks or so, and she's going to be spending the first couple of days at my mom's house. Typically, on Christmas Eve we go to my mom's house for dinner and open gifts at midnight. Since Gianna is little and doesn't make it till midnight no matter how hard she tries, we usually let her open a bunch right after dinner. We spend the night so we have brunch the following morning, and Gianna opens the gifts from Santa then.

This year, she will already be there. I'm just going to meet her there when I go on Christmas Eve, which falls on a Thursday this year.

I flick my wrist and check the time on my watch. "She should be here any minute, baby girl."

As those words leave my mouth, the doorbell rings. Gianna and I exchange looks. She's smiling widely at me.

"See, there's your auntie right there. Go grab your teddy and backpack."

"Yay!" Gianna leaps off the couch and heads into her room to grab her bag and teddy bear. She never leaves to spend the night without that thing. She's had it since she was a baby and sleeps with it every single night. She gives the phrase "attached at the hip" new meaning.

I walk to the door and open it. To my surprise, it's not Marianna.

Carissa stands in front of me wearing a dazzling smile, and my God, does she look breathtaking in her tight red dress... She's wearing a sparkling red lipstick that matches her dress, making her lips look even better than they typically do. *Luscious Lips...*

"Carissa, hi." I smile, genuinely delighted to see her, but I totally forgot she was going to be here so soon. I stand in between the door and its frame, leaving it barely cracked. Shit, where's Marianna? She was supposed to have picked up Gianna by now.

"Hi. I hope I'm not too early. I wanted to beat traffic, so I left a little bit earlier than I was intending to."

"No, no. You're fine," I respond, still captivated by the way she looks. Damn...

Her smile starts to fade, and a confused expression graces her face. "Uh, can I come in?"

I shake my head, snapping out of my daze. "Oh, yeah... Of course, I'm sorry." I step out of the way so she can walk in.

Before she does, she looks past me and stops dead in her tracks. "Hi, you must be Gianna. I'm Carissa."

I snap my head to the left, and standing next to me is my little girl with her backpack sitting on her shoulders and her teddy bear clutched closely to her chest.

I wasn't planning on introducing Gianna to Carissa, at least not for a long time. I'm very overprotective of my daughter, and anything I do has her best interests in mind. I don't know if introducing her to someone I'm seeing—especially when I'm not sure if it's going to lead anywhere—is such a good idea. Are we technically even seeing each other? We've only just started hanging out a few times.

I gently place a hand behind Gianna's back and nudge her forward. "Go on. Be polite. Say hello to daddy's *friend*, Carissa." Was I supposed to call her that?

Gianna brings a finger up to her mouth and whispers, "Hello."

Carissa looks back at me and smiles. "She's so precious."

I smile back. "Thank you, come on in."

She walks in, and I close the door behind her. As she makes her way into the living room and places her coat and purse onto the couch, Gianna stays close to me. She's shy when she doesn't know someone. Plus, we're not used to having new people over.

"Wow, that smells incredible," she says.

"Thanks, it should be just about done."

I pick up some of Gianna's toys from the living room and try to apologize. "Please excuse the mess. I'm sorry, my sister should be here any moment to pick her up. She's running late at work." I sit on the arm of the couch and Gianna places herself in between my legs.

Carissa smiles. "It's not a problem, really. I'm happy I got to meet her. I know how important she is to you."

I nod, but is it possible for her to already know just how much Gianna really means to me?

"Can I get you something to drink?" I ask, searching her big brown eyes. Damn... gorgeous.

She shakes her head. "No, I'm good, thanks."

Carissa's gaze wanders back to my daughter, and I can tell she wants to say something. Just as she opens her mouth, the ringing of the doorbell stops her.

"Okay, now that's Aunt Mari," I say to Gianna. She's trying to hide her smile as her eyes flash back to Carissa.

I chuckle softly and carefully move her to the side so I can answer the door. "Hang on, sweetheart."

As I open the door wide for Marianna, she barges in without noticing Carissa. "I'm so sorry! I tried to leave on time, but this time of the year is absolutely nuts. Wow, the food smells amazing! What did you—" Marianna's eyes meet with Carissa's, and I just stand back watching. "Oh, I'm sorry. Hi, I'm Marianna, Lorenzo's sister." She steps forward, extending her hand.

I had already told Marianna I had a date with Carissa tonight, but I was hoping not to have to introduce them to one another. Not yet anyway.

Carissa's radiant smile lights up the room. "Hi, nice to meet you. I'm Carissa."

I'm never going to hear the end of this once I'm alone with Marianna on Christmas Eve.

"Auntie Mari!" Gianna shouts, throwing herself at my sister.

Marianna lifts Gianna up into her arms. "Hi, princess!" She places kisses on both of her cheeks. "Are you ready to go?"

Gianna nods fiercely a couple of times. "Yes! I'm ready!"

Marianna smiles. "Okay, go on and say bye-bye to Daddy."

"Okay."

Marianna places Gianna back down on the ground. My daughter comes darting at me, and I pick her up.

"Bye, Daddy!"

I give her a kiss and hold her tight. "Bye, sweetheart. Be

good for Nonno, Nonna, Aunt Mari, and Uncle Maxy. I'll see you in a couple of days."

"Okay, Daddy." I place her down, and she goes straight for my sister's hand. "Come on, Auntie Mari, let's go."

"Okay, let's go," Marianna repeats. She looks at Carissa and says, "It was nice meeting you. I'm sorry, she's in a rush to go."

Carissa shifts her weight from one foot to the other. "Oh, it's fine. It was very nice meeting you too. Bye, Gianna."

"Bye," Gianna answers, finally smiling at Carissa. That smile right there tells me she likes her. That's a damn relief for me.

Once they're out the door and on their way, I lock it and turn around to face Carissa. "I'm so sorry. My daughter is always ready for the next big thing. Plus, she loves going over to my parents' house and hanging out with them and my siblings."

She chuckles softly. "It's okay, really. She is adorable. Your sister seems very nice too."

"She can be a real pain in the ass," I say, shrugging.

She laughs. "Aren't all sisters?"

I nod. "True that." I remember her telling me things her older sister used to do to her when they were growing up. They were all jokes, and Carissa would do the same to her sister at any chance she got, but since Carissa was younger, her sister got her a hell of a lot more.

"Please, have a seat." I motion toward the couch.

We sit fairly close to one another, and the sudden urge to kiss her—the one I felt last time we were together—comes rushing back. Sure, I was in awe of her when I first saw her, but I think because Gianna was here, it was holding me back from feeling what I am now... how much I want this woman, right here on my couch.

Damn, where the hell did that come from? I've been very physically attracted to her since the first moment I saw her, but actually considering touching her is something new… at least admitting it to myself is. I've wanted to kiss her for a while. I've thought about it plenty of times, and I've come close to doing it. But now, admitting to myself that I want her right here and right now, that's something new.

And I want her in every sense of the word. If this were back in the day before I met Sylvia, I would have made a move on Carissa already. I would have taken her into my arms and kissed her fiercely, lying her back on this couch.

But not today. Today, I'm reserved, and although Lord knows I want to make a move, I won't do it.

"So, are you still close to her mother?" Carissa asks, bringing me out of my very inappropriate thoughts.

I furrow my brows. "Whose mother?"

"Your daughter's?"

Oh, crap. That's right. We never discussed *her mother*, my late wife. I'm not used to someone addressing Sylvia as just Gianna's mother. It was always *your wife…* even though she's gone. Addressing her as just Gianna's mother seems like we're no longer together, not that she's passed away. Of course Carissa is assuming Sylvia and I broke up. Any normal person wouldn't automatically assume someone else has passed away.

I swallow hard and take a deep breath.

Carissa takes notice and her expression changes. "I'm sorry. I didn't mean to pry. I was just—"

"No, no. It's fine." I struggle with finding my next words, but somehow, I make it through without bringing myself to tears. "Her mother, *my wife…* She passed away when Gianna was just a baby."

Carissa's mouth forms an O as she gasps. "Oh, I'm sorry. I didn't know."

I shake my head. "You couldn't have… I don't typically bring her up in conversation. I had a hard time pushing through it for the longest time…"

She nods. "I can understand that. It seems you did great with Gianna."

A small smile forms on my face. "Thanks. I had a lot of help from my family."

"It's great they're there for you."

I nod. "I don't know where I would be without them."

She smiles, not saying anything further.

I stand and say, "Hey, I think it's just about done. Why don't you make yourself comfortable, and I'll see if it's ready."

"Okay, sounds good."

"That was delicious. Have you always been such a wonderful cook?" Carissa asks with a smile.

I take a sip of wine and shake my head. "Definitely not. I learned a few things once I became a daddy. Since I live here alone with my daughter, I need to make sure I feed her good, nutritious food. You can thank my mother for that recipe."

She laughs. "Maybe I will."

Her words have a lot more meaning than I realized before I heard them. *Maybe she will...*

She'd have to meet my mother for it to happen, or talk to her on the phone. Either way, it's a lot.

Maybe it's too much.

But maybe it's time.

As we sit on the couch in the living room of my place, I lean in a bit closer to her. I know it's either now or never. If I'm not ready to do this now, will I ever be?

I need to take the next step, see if this thing is even worth trying for.

But is there a point to this? Why am I trying to find love again? Is that even what I'm doing? At this point, I don't know. I don't have any of those answers.

All I do know is whenever I'm not with this woman, she's

always on my mind. Sometimes it's pure and innocent thoughts, like how sweet she is and how much we seem to be getting along.

But other times?

Other times she makes me think of things I want to do to her, with her, that I haven't done in so long. Things I haven't wanted to do ever since my wife died.

It's been five long, hard years, but now, I'm starting to feel them again. Now I'm coming to life.

And it has to be because of her.

I know this is all new for her too. She's told me plenty of times her ex screwed her up and she's been against dating since it ended between them.

There's something about when she's with me or when we're talking on the phone. I feel an instant connection, an instant chemistry between us.

Her eyes tell me she wants me too. The way she's staring at me with those bedroom eyes… I have to go for it.

"Carissa," I whisper.

"Yes?" she replies in the same low tone.

I continue leaning closer, and now she's doing the same. I point upward, and her eyes follow my finger. Above us is the mistletoe Gianna insisted we buy for our home and place directly above the couch.

Her eyes come back to mine, and I can't stop myself from wrapping my arms around her.

Bam. Our lips come together in a gentle crash of emotions.

After so long, after seeing her and coming so close to doing it just before pulling myself away, I'm finally letting it all go and kissing the one woman who I can't seem to get my mind off of.

This has nothing to do with the mistletoe. Were it not there, I still would have kissed her.

And now, the nickname I'd given her when I first saw her, Luscious Lips, also has new meaning.

Damn, they're perfect.

Damn, they're soft.

Damn, I can't get enough.

I feel her writhing in my embrace as a soft moan escapes her.

Jesus fucking Christ. She's making it really hard for me to hold back and only kiss her.

However, it's all I do, and she continues yearning for me.

We kiss softly for the next couple of minutes until I pull away. I pull away not because I'm afraid or because I want to stop kissing her.

No, it's quite the opposite.

If I didn't stop when I did, I would have wanted to go further.

Damn, hearing her sexy moans is only intensifying every single thought I've ever had of her as I'd lie in bed every night. The hard-on in my jeans confirms it.

Kissing her is everything I imagined it would be. Kissing her made me want her even more than I thought before, and now I want to take that next step with her.

I do.

I truly do. My dick is pure indication of it, and if I were wearing sweatpants, I'm sure she'd notice it too.

But the next step is not one I'm ready to take. Not yet anyway. Maybe someday.

As our lips part and we pull back from one another, we both smile, but my arms never let her go.

We spend the evening on my couch, kissing innocently and nothing more until it's time for her to go home.

Chapter Sixteen

LORENZO

"Man, I really thought this year, she would have made it," Marianna says to me, pointing at Gianna who is cuddled up against me on the couch. She's holding on tightly to one of the new dolls she received tonight.

I chuckle. "Well, she definitely tried."

It's just after midnight, and we opened all the presents not long ago. Now I'm sitting with my sister in my parents' living room while Max is in the other room finishing the rest of the pie with Mom and Dad.

Marianna sits back against the couch as she swirls the wine in her cup. Then she flashes me a knowing look.

Oh shit, here we go.

"So, Carissa, huh?"

Damn. As soon as she says her name, the taste and feel of her lips against mine are all I can think about. Fuck, I miss kissing her.

I miss her.

I shake the thoughts from my head before Marianna can pick up that I'm daydreaming about Carissa.

I knew it was too good to be true that she'd let me off the

hook about it. She had just been waiting for a moment to get me alone.

"Carissa," I reply with a smile.

Marianna chuckles. "She's very pretty, and Gianna seemed to like her."

I nod. "Yes, she is," I say, referring to Carissa being pretty. "And yes, she did."

Marianna takes a sip from her cup. After she swallows, she says, "I kept my promise. I haven't told Max."

And for it, I'm grateful.

"Thanks, sis. I'm going to be telling him soon… especially since things with her have been going so well."

"Oh, have they?" she asks teasingly.

I smirk. "Shut up."

Marianna looks away and downs the rest of her drink. Then she looks back at me and looks away once more.

"Hey, everything okay?" I ask as she stares into deep space. I can take one guess as to what this is about.

She meets my gaze once more, and now there are tears welling in her eyes.

"Awww, Mari. What's going on? Talk to me." I already know what it is, but I don't want to just put it out there in case she doesn't really want to tell me.

Marianna shrugs. "It's Christmas Eve. This is supposed to be the time of year when you're surrounded by family… you know, *the most wonderful time of the year?* But it's not for me." She shrugs and swallows hard. "Sure, I do my best to hold my head up and *act* like it doesn't bother me, but can you tell me where my husband is? Because I wouldn't be able to. I don't have the slightest idea."

I shake my head slowly, in disbelief of what she's telling me. At the same time, I knew it had something to do with Jordan not being around. "Isn't he in Cali on business?" I'm praying to God that's where he is, because if he's not where he told my sister he was going to be, he's got a serious death wish. I still don't understand why people want to test the UFC heavyweight champion.

"*Is he?* I have no idea. He hasn't called me in days." She places her cup on the coffee table in front of her and refills it with the bottle of wine once more.

"Days?" I'm gonna kill this motherfucker.

She chuckles, but she's not finding this at all funny. I can tell by the murderous expression on her face because, just like me, my sister also has a bit of a temper. Of course, it's nowhere near the same as mine, but it's enough. She's just waiting for the perfect moment. "I lost count of how many." She throws the drink back and swallows as soon as it hits her throat.

I take a good look at my sister. I don't know why this piece of shit is treating her this way. She's been nothing but a great wife to him since before they even got married.

"Mari, what are you going to do?" She should leave his ass. She shouldn't take any more of his shit. This isn't the first time he's done something like this to her. The last time he cheated on her was before they got married, and she forgave him. I'd held him up by his collar against the wall, and she begged me not to hurt him.

Because she knew I was two seconds away from rear-ranging his face.

Asshole.

Anyway, she forgave him, they moved on from it, and they got married. Two years later and he's at it again. It makes me wonder if he's been untruthful and unfaithful for longer than we've known.

Marianna shrugs and once again downs the rest of her drink. "What can I do?"

"You know exactly what you need to do. He's not treating you right."

She stares at me without saying a word, but I know she knows exactly what she needs to do this time.

Minutes later, she takes a deep breath, nodding. "Look, don't say anything to Mom, Dad, or Max, okay? I haven't said anything yet. I don't want them to worry, but I'll tell them. I just need some time and the holidays to pass."

I nod in agreement. "I won't say anything, but hasn't anyone else asked about him?"

She shrugs. "Of course they have, but like always, I've been making excuses for him. I just know he's cheating on me again." Marianna looks away just as Max walks in.

Guess it's time to change the direction of the conversation.

My eyes dart toward him. "Hey, man." I wave two fingers in the air.

"Yo, I'm stuffed," Max announces, taking a seat on one of the couches.

"You finally finished shoving pie down your throat?" I ask. Max is known for eating a few pieces of pie every year on Christmas Eve. It's like his own personal holiday tradition.

"Hey, Mom makes the best pies around. You can't say no when she brings them out," he says.

"That's true." My mother does make the best apple, blueberry, chocolate mousse, and key lime pies in the world.

"She fell asleep?" he asks, pointing at Gianna.

I nod, picking her up and rising to my feet. "I'm about to put her to bed."

Marianna finally looks toward us, her eyes obviously red. "I think I'm going to bed too. Night, fellas." She gets to her feet and darts out of the room before either of us have a chance to answer.

"Damn, I can't take it anymore," Max says.

I adjust Gianna in my arms. "Can't take what anymore?"

He scoffs. "She hasn't said anything to me, but I'm not blind. I know what's going on, and I personally have an ill taste for Jordan. He's messing with the wrong family."

Of course he knows. My sister tries her hardest to not worry the family, but being that we are so closely knit, there's no way any of us wouldn't notice when something like this is going on. I'm pretty sure my parents know too.

"Man, she promised me not to say anything, but I had a horrible feeling about it."

He shrugs. "I just want to know why she hasn't told me, like does she think I'm not trustworthy enough or what?"

I chuckle. "No one tells you anything because you're quick to snap… a family trait, I guess. But when you snap, it's always trouble. Plus, you're quick to tell Mom and Dad everything."

"Man, that was so long ago! And not for nothing, but you're the one with the temper, Mr. UFC Heavyweight Champion." He laughs.

I laugh along with him. "Well, bro. I have something to tell you too, but it's going to have to wait. I've got to get this little one into bed. Have a good night." I walk toward the door with Gianna in my arms.

"Wait! What's up? Tell me now," he says.

I spin around to face him with a smirk. "I'll tell you soon. Night-night, li'l bro."

He grimaces playfully. "Night, Enz." Moments later, he calls out to me again. "Hey, Enz?"

"Yeah?"

He shrugs. "Guess I'm playing Santa Max again," he says, pointing at the milk and cookies set on the coffee table. The colorful, sparkling lights of the Christmas tree reflect off the glass.

I chuckle. "Yup. Make sure you finish them all and place the gifts under the tree and in the stockings. She'll be up by five tomorrow morning, so get to it."

Max rubs his belly. "I'm so going to get a stomachache."

"Better you than me, li'l bro," I say jokingly.

"Hey, Enz?"

"Yeah?"

He puts up his middle finger. "Merry Christmas."

I laugh. "Merry Christmas, fucker."

I snap my eyes open to the sunlight coming in through the small cracks in the blinds. The New York Yankees posters and decals still line the walls. I find it hilarious how my mom has yet to change my room around, even though I've been out of the house for years. She's got all my old trophies and books sitting on the shelves. My gaming chair is set off to the side in front of the television set from my teenage years. I don't think I've played a video game since I left home.

I'm surprised Gianna is not up yet and running full speed toward me, begging me to open all the gifts from Santa. I look toward my left at the nightstand and find my cell phone. I pick it up; it's just after six in the morning.

Is it too early to text someone and wish them Merry Christmas? Because I have this itching sensation to text Carissa already.

I freaking miss talking to her.

It's Christmas. She's probably up with her family opening gifts, isn't she?

I take a shot and compose a text to her. Hopefully she's not still asleep and won't curse me out for waking her up.

Me: Merry Christmas, beautiful.

I wallow in self-pity after five minutes go by and she still hasn't responded. She's totally going to curse me out when she gets this.

Another ten minutes go by, and finally, she responds back.

Carissa: Merry Christmas, sexy ;)

A smile forms across my face. She thinks I'm sexy. I think she's sexy as fuck. Do I dare ask her for a picture right now? Nothing scandalous, of course. I just want to see her pretty face and gorgeous smile.

Me: I miss you... send me a picture of your pretty face... please?

She replies with a smiley face emoji followed by a picture of her in scrubs. Still, she's damn gorgeous. Before I have a chance to reply, she texts me again.

Carissa: And I miss you, too, by the way. I keep thinking about kissing you...

Oh, this could be so dangerous. My cock stirs to life. Fuck.

Me: You don't know how badly I wanna kiss you again, too.

Me: You are so beautiful... is that pic from now?

Carissa: Yeah, I'm at work... early shift. No holidays off for the hospital crew ;)

Damn, I didn't even think about if she might be working. But it's true. Doctors and hospital staff rarely have off on holidays. I know she's not a doctor or nurse, but in order to run the hospital, they have to have their staff present, even if only a few of them at a time.

> **Me: So, you know what I'm going to ask you now, right?**
>
> **Carissa: What's that?**
>
> **Me: I wanna see you again. Come by my house tomorrow night? Let me cook for you again. You work too hard… come by my place, chill out on the couch, and I'll rub your feet for you :)**
>
> **Carissa: That sounds wonderful. I'll be there.**

Smiling again, I think of Carissa laid out on my couch in some sexy pj's while I rub her down. Damn, I need to stop.

I text her back to find out what time works for her, and we set a date for seven again.

Perfect. I can't wait to see her. Getting through this day is going to drag.

"Daddy!" I hear Gianna's screaming voice as she jumps onto my bed and wraps her arms around me.

Actually, I think I'm going to really enjoy today until it's time to see Carissa again.

"Merry Christmas, sweetheart," I say, placing kisses on her head.

"Daddy! Santa came! Come, let's go open presents!"

"She burst into my room, tugging on my sleeve. Get up, Enz," Max says from my doorway, rubbing his eyes. Knowing him, he probably got to bed late and now is in desperate need of an espresso.

Marianna walks up behind him and peeks in. "Merry Christmas, guys."

"Merry Christmas," I reply. I gently move Gianna over and say, "Okay, let Daddy get up, and I'll meet you in the living room. Go with Uncle Maxy and Auntie Mari to see if

Nonno and Nonna are up." I know my parents are already up. They're in the kitchen having coffee. This is just what they do.

"Okay, Daddy!" Gianna shouts excitedly, jumping off the bed. She darts toward my brother and sister and grabs them both by the hand. "Come on, Uncle Maxy and Auntie Mari! Let's go!"

I smile as the three of them head down the hall.

It's going to be a good day.

Chapter Seventeen

CARISSA

I don't know what's been going on with me. One minute I'm holding back, not trying to fall for his charming good looks, amazing personality, and humungous biceps. Yes, I said it... humungous biceps that drive me crazy whenever he wraps his arms around me. And the next minute, I'm really liking him.

Like, super really liking him.

Like on the verge of falling in love with him.

It scares me. God, does it scare the shit out of me. I haven't been here in so long, and I swore up and down, left and right, and all ways possible that I would never do it again after the way things ended with Steve.

"So things are good?" Daniela asks me through the phone, bringing me back to reality.

I'm currently throwing on some jeans, getting ready to leave the house to see Lorenzo tonight. The nerves in my belly have been going wild all day long. I'm so nervous, and excited, and anxious, and, oh my God, every good and nerve-wracking emotion possible.

I step back and take in my reflection in the mirror,

141

cocking my head to one side. "Yeah, girl. Things have actually been *so* good… like it scares me."

She chuckles. "Yo, you're falling for him. *Hard.*"

Falling…

I'm afraid I may have already fallen.

I sit on the edge of my bed and look out toward the window. "Yeah, I realized that this morning when I first woke up. It hit me… like lightning, and since then, I've been scared shitless. But at the same time, it's kind of nice." I shrug.

"Of course it is, girl! After the shit you've been through with Steve? You deserve everything good. And why not with a super-hot guy who's a UFC Heavyweight Champion?" She chuckles. "Oh my God. I still can't believe you're dating Lorenzo Trevano. Do you know how many women would kill to be in your shoes? Me included."

I let out a short laugh. "I guess. I mean, yeah, it's awesome he's this hotshot, but the part of it that makes it the best of all is he's this super sweet guy… like no joke. And he's a great dad. His daughter is the cutest thing around with big blue eyes and long dark curls. She seriously looks like a porcelain doll."

"I wasn't even aware he had a daughter. How old is she again?" she asks.

"Five." Thoughts of the day I met Gianna come crashing into the front of my mind. She is so precious. To think, Lorenzo is raising her all on his own. He did so well. Okay, yes, he said he has family to help, but I'm sure they're not always around. He lives alone with her, so when she's sick or wakes up in the middle of the night from a nightmare, he's the one there for her. He's the one who cooks and takes care of her mostly.

But if this thing with him goes any further… If he and I actually get to the next step with one another, will I be able to fill the shoes of stepmother? Yeah, I know I'm thinking way ahead in the future and it would mean we're married, but I have to consider it as a possibility, maybe. I have to take it into consideration because being with someone who already has a child is important. I know Gianna means the world to him, so if he's going to be with me, he's trusting me to be around her and with her. And that, I know, is the most important thing to him.

Will I be able to be a mother?

I've always wanted kids and have pictured my life as one day becoming a mom, but it was under different circumstances. I'd be married and my husband and I would have a kid together. I never imagined I'd be with someone who already has a daughter from a previous relationship.

Or marriage.

I can't believe he was married. Am I ever going to measure up to who his wife was? I know nothing about her, but I can only imagine how hard it was on him when she passed. Is this something I want to get myself into? Am I ready to give my heart to someone who's loved and lost someone so dear to him?

I rise from the bed and leave the bedroom. If I want to be on time, I need to hurry, and my hair still needs help. I enter the bathroom and wrap my first section onto the curling iron. Good thing I had turned it on a few minutes ago, and thank God for AirPods. Knowing me, I probably would end up burning myself if I had to be on the phone and use the iron at the same time.

"See, that is amazing. I'm so happy for you, girl. If I thought he was no good, I would have told you. But he's a great guy, so I'm telling you to go for it. You're only scared because of what happened in your past relationships. You will overcome it once you keep getting to know him."

Do I tell her I'm also scared because I feel I may not be enough due to him loving someone else a long time ago? No, probably not. It's a discussion for another time. I place another section of hair around the iron and hold it steady for a few seconds. I take the conversation to safer grounds than my thoughts. "And that's the thing, Dani... I feel like I've known him for so long."

"Damn, I miss being in love and feeling that way." She lets out a soft chuckle. "Anyway, I have to run, girl. I'm about to start my shift. Are you coming in tomorrow?"

"Yeah, I'll be there."

"Okay, I'll see you then. Text me later with details!"

I chuckle. "Will do. Bye, girl."

We hang up the phone, and I continue fixing my hair. Another fifteen minutes or so and I should be all ready to go.

I swallow thickly and step out of the car. The time has finally come to see him, and I've been considering turning right back around and going home.

I adjust the hood attached to my coat as a light snow begins to fall. Good thing I'm wearing my boots.

Something about tonight feels different. Something about tonight feels like things are moving. In the right direction? Maybe. I don't know for sure. All I do know is I'm happy and scared at the same time.

How is it possible to feel such a difference of emotions with so much passion simultaneously?

I never imagined I'd be at this spot in my life again. If someone would have told me two months ago that on the day after Christmas I'd be going to a guy's house for the second time and that we'd already kissed—damn, I can't wait to taste those sexy lips of his again—I would have said they were crazy and out of their mind. There was no way I'd go back down this road after what happened with Steve.

I mean, we were going to be married, and he killed me. He destroyed me and everything I had ever believed in when it came to love. I placed chains and brick walls around my heart the moment he took off.

Yet, here I am now, ready to dive headfirst with my eyes closed. When it comes to love, diving in blind tends to be what happens because the person entrusted with a heart can just as easily destroy it.

Like Steve destroyed me. I was dead inside for years.

But somehow, someway, Lorenzo "Guns" Trevano awoke me. He broke through the icy-cold box I placed around my heart and completely melted it away.

And now, I'm standing on his doorstep while snow comes down around me.

I ring the bell. Butterflies in my stomach are fluttering away aimlessly.

It's just after seven in the evening on the day after Christmas, and all day I was counting down the moments till I'd see him again.

Forget butterflies. These are moths and dragonflies, and they're wild. The nerves in the pit of my belly are doing somersaults.

Any minute now, he's going to come open this door, and everything I've been feeling up to this point will go away. He'll make it all better.

"Carissa, you're here." Lorenzo smiles as he opens the door.

"Are you sure you don't want me to help with that? I don't mind, really." I stand a few feet from Lorenzo as he rinses the dishes and pots from dinner.

It was a fantastic meal once again. Gianna is lucky to have a dad who can cook for her, and from what he's told me, she can eat—especially his mother's cooking.

He shakes his head. "Nope. You just stand right there,

looking all cute, and I'll be happy."

I blush. *"Looking all cute...* you're too much." I take a sip from my glass. I've noticed that since I've been seeing him, my alcohol tolerance has definitely gone up. I used to not care for it. Now, I crave it. Maybe it's compensation for craving him.

I have been thinking about being with him intimately since the night we kissed. I want to kiss him again. And I want him kissing me... all over.

He turns off the water and picks up a dish rag to dry his hands. "Yup. *Looking all cute* and gorgeous." He takes a deep breath, letting his eyes roam over me, which ultimately land back on my lips. "And luscious."

I giggle. *"Luscious?"* My core is beginning to ache with want—need. Why is he making it so hard for me to cool off? At this rate, I'm going to be humping the walls as soon as I get home. Plus, him wearing gray sweatpants is not making this any easier on me.

He chuckles and breaks his stare. Then, coming back toward me, he says, "Don't get mad at me, okay?"

I furrow my brows, still smiling. "What? Why? What are you talking about?"

"Nah, forget it. You'll probably hate me for this." He looks down at the ground.

Yeah, right. I could never hate him. "No, I won't. Tell me." I take a sip of the champagne from my glass.

Lorenzo looks back at my lips and meets my gaze. He shrugs. "I used to call you Luscious Lips before we officially met and I knew your name."

I almost spit out my drink. "What?!"

"See, I told you. You hate me." He turns around but then flips back and lowers his head.

I chuckle. "No, I don't. I think it's kind of funny, actually. But you have to tell me why and your reasoning." Shit, feeling the way I'm feeling right now, with my core all tingling, I definitely want to hear all about why he called me Luscious Lips.

He leans in closer and wraps his arms around me, sending me into a frenzy. Shit, I want him even more now.

His eyes hood over, and his stare takes my breath away. "Well, isn't it obvious? You have *the most* luscious lips I've ever seen and, since the other day, the most luscious lips I've ever had the pleasure of tasting." His voice lowers to the sexiest tone I've ever heard, and his mouth is now just inches from mine. "And I want to taste them once more."

I swallow thickly. "I want you to taste them again too."

I place my glass on the counter in just enough time. Before I know it, our lips crash together like they did that night.

He tastes so good.

He tastes fucking amazing, and all I want to do is rip his damn clothes off.

As if reading my mind, he kisses my neck and quickly lifts me and sets me on top of the counter, knocking my glass to the floor.

In this moment, I don't even care about the clatter that it makes. All that matters are his lips against mine.

It wets my jeans before it goes down, but it doesn't matter. I don't stop him, and he keeps going.

He continues placing his mouth along the length of my neck as his hands roam frantically along my body.

I don't stop him. In fact, I welcome him by responding to his every touch.

"Carissa..." he whispers, then drives his tongue into my mouth.

As he moves his lips back to my neck and his hand explores my breasts over my shirt, a soft moan escapes me. "Lorenzo... God, this feels so good."

"You haven't seen anything yet."

Holy hell, what? I love the way that sounds.

He places his hands under my ass and stills. He must feel the wet spot from the remnants of the champagne. "Fuck, I'm sorry... I didn't realize."

"I don't care. Please don't stop," I beg.

"Are you sure?" He searches my eyes and then reaches for a towel to help dry me off.

I grab his arm, stopping him. "Yes, I don't care. Hell, take them off me. Please." I kick off my boots, and they land to the ground in a thud.

His eyes widen, and he thinks only for a moment before unbuttoning and unzipping my jeans. My pussy is calling out to him as he helps me out of my pants and his hands caress my thighs.

Lorenzo throws my jeans to the side and stares down at my most intimate section: my drenched panties. They're not drenched from the champagne. They're drenched because of everything he's doing to me and making me feel. A small smile pulls at the corners of his lips.

He looks up at me, as if asking if it's okay to touch, and even though I'm feeling a little self-conscious right now, I nod. "Go ahead. Touch me, Lorenzo."

He places two fingers over my area, and they circle the wet spot, then he bites down on his bottom lip. "Fuck, Carissa..."

My eyes close when his lips come back to meet mine. While we kiss, he lifts me into his arms and my legs automatically wrap around his waist.

He carries me out of the kitchen, our lips never parting.

He tastes so good.

So fucking good.

Like alcohol and candy.

Like heaven and hell at the same damn time, and I'm not ready to be brought back to Earth.

Fuck. I don't ever want to come back to Earth.

I snap my eyes open the moment he crashes us onto his

bed. Frantically, we remove each other's clothes—well, the rest of mine. I only have my shirt and panties left.

As he slips my shirt up over my head, he growls, and Lord is it sexy. I can't wait to hear his growls as he's pleasing me and mid-orgasm. I help him unhook my bra and let him fling it off. Then he throws it to the side, off the bed.

"My God... Mmmm," he says, bringing his mouth onto my breasts, taking in an erect nipple.

"Jesus, Lorenzo," I moan loudly, snapping my head back and hitting the pillow.

"Fuck, sweetheart. You're so damn sexy," he says, coming up for air. "So fucking sexy as hell... damn." He goes back and takes my other nipple into his mouth.

My knees shake. I desperately need my pussy to be rubbed any way possible. He's killing me right now.

I reach down to grab the corners of his shirt and pull it up over his head. It forces him to let go of my nipple from between his teeth, but I want him naked more than anything else right now. I toss it to the side because I don't care where it lands. I just want to feel him and be as close to him as possible.

As he moves back, I see his insanely muscled form. His pecs are defined. His abs form an eight pack. He's a complete god. Of course, this isn't the first time I'm seeing him without a shirt on, but it is the first time I'm close enough to touch him.

Feel him.

Taste him. Yum. I can't wait to wrap my tongue around the rest of him.

I place my hands behind his neck and pull him closer to me, making his lips crash into mine once more. I never want his lips to leave my body. He's allowed to kiss other parts of me of course, but he's definitely not allowed to take them off of me.

He sucks on my bottom lip, and the sensation is completely insane.

"Fuck, I love your lips so damn much, Carissa."

"Yeah? Well, I can't wait to put them on you." I reach down and tug on his sweats. They need to come off this instant.

"Carissa, wait," he whispers as he pulls away from me.

Breathless, I respond. "What? What is it?" I wasn't ready to stop tasting him, and I don't want to talk right now. It's been too long since I've felt anything even remotely as good as this. Stopping now is not an option.

"I just want to make sure you're okay with all of this. I mean, I think you are, but—"

I grab the top part of his pants again. "If you don't help me get these things off of you this instant, I'm going to flip you over and have my way with you."

A sexy smirk forms on his face. He's obviously pleased with my answer. "Maybe I would love for you to do that."

"Maybe I'll make your wish come true then." Without giving him another second to think, I slide up from under him and push him onto his bed by the shoulders. He could have easily stopped me, considering his size, but I had a feeling he would gladly let me.

He lays his head on the pillow, allowing me to get to work. Damn, I haven't done this in so long. I sure as hell hope I don't suck right now.

Well, I will *suck*, but not suck… Oh, forget it. My thoughts are getting to me, and I just need to relax and get down to business.

I take a deep breath and pull his pants down in one swift movement. The fact that he's wearing nothing else underneath has not escaped me. It's damn sexy when his cock springs out.

My mouth goes agape, taking in his size. "Wow." I chuckle.

Quickly snapping his head up to look at me, he says, "Ugh. Is that bad?"

My eyes widen, and I move my gaze away from his cock. I trace it with my fingertips, enjoying the way it feels. "Quite the contrary... you're freaking huge!"

His smile returns, and he lays his head back down. "Phew... you had me worried for a second."

"If you're worried about having a python, a lot of guys are in trouble then. You're the largest I've ever seen—had. Damn..."

I haven't been around the block too many times, but I've had my share of guys throughout my life. I can absolutely say they would have killed to be this big. Can you say porn star?

I lean down and get to work, placing my lips on his cock and opening wide to take in his whole length.

He grunts. "Fuck, Carissa! You've got some amazing lips and an even better mouth... mmmm."

I smile with him still in my mouth and continue working him, and as I do, I feel him growing even more inside my mouth. I thought he was big before... Shit, I'm in trouble.

I hear his low moans and grunts as he helps me by gently rocking his hips in my direction. He places his hands on my head, but he's delicate and doesn't shove his cock further down my throat like one would think a UFC fighter might do, since they're known for being such tough guys. But Lorenzo is gentle.

Minutes later, he places his hands on my shoulders. "Carissa... Oh my God, you're so fucking good at that, I'm gonna blow. Wait... wait—"

I'm about to tell him that's the whole point, but before I have a chance to do so, he lifts me and places me on my back instead.

He looks incredible right now, like something I'd see if I were watching what the perfect anatomy of a man should look like. The perfection of him is beyond belief. The way each indentation and hard line complements the next is something fierce.

He places himself between my legs and peppers soft kisses on my thighs and pussy. "Do you…" Kiss. Kiss. "Know how…" Kiss. Kiss. "Hard that was…" Kiss. Kiss. "For me…" Kiss. Kiss. "To stop you…" Kiss. Kiss. "While you were sucking me?" Kiss. Kiss. Kiss.

I chuckle but, at the same time, writhe as he's teasing me.

He lifts his head and looks into my eyes. I bring a hand down and caress his hair. Damn, he's so beautiful.

He smiles and closes his eyes for a second. Then, he goes back to placing kisses over my panties. "God, I love the sweet smell of you," he murmurs, hooking two fingers around the strap on the sides. "It's my turn to make you quiver and shake."

"Oh, damn…" I coo as he pulls my panties down.

I lift my hips, helping him get me completely naked because I can't wait any longer to have him inside of me. The crazy buildup and anticipation to feel him inside me is more than I can bear right now.

This is not the longest I've held out before. I made Steve wait six months before even letting him finger me. I wasn't as comfortable with him as I am with Lorenzo—but this is definitely harder. Waiting to be intimate with Lorenzo has been difficult because he's constantly on my mind, and something about the way he looks at me every single time we're together drives me absolutely crazy.

His eyes are so sexy with how they bore into me. I can't help but think of sex every time he looks at me this way.

"Damn, baby. I can hear your kitty purring for me," he says as two of his fingers graze my slit.

I moan. "Lorenzo."

His fingers brush my area three more times before he finally inserts them inside me.

"Oh my God!" I scream, bucking my hips. The thousands

of sensations flowing through my body make my head snap back.

"Fuck, Carissa," he whispers before whipping his tongue up and down my clit.

Oh my fucking God. I'm going to touch the stars.

I whip my head back and forth, writhing from the feeling, and spread my legs further, but no matter how wide I try to move them, they're still not far enough apart.

He alternates between suckles and licks, and it's barely two minutes of pleasure when my peak hits, and I come crashing down.

"Oh, God!" I push his head away because I can't take the way it feels anymore. I'm just too damn sensitive.

I squeeze my knees together, but as I do, he sits up and parts them with his hands. "Oh, no. I'm not done with you yet," he says with a devilish smirk.

I'm not ready for anything more. That was so intense after not having any for years. I don't think I can take any more of what he has to give me.

Slowly, he lowers himself on top of me and pushes a strand of hair out of my eyes. "You're so fucking beautiful, Carissa."

His lips come down onto mine, and that's when he pushes himself deep inside me.

"I'm going to go slow, baby, so I don't hurt you. It's been too long for both of us," he whispers in my ear, softly pushing in and out of me.

"Okay," I coo.

As he keeps going, his thrusts intensify, and now I'm starting to feel his entire dick forcing its way farther into me.

It's feeling so good.

So damn good, I'm on the verge of crying. Fuck.

I claw his back and grip onto him tightly. He's massive and is stretching me out completely.

"Oh my fucking GOD!" I whip my head to the side.

"Jesus, you're so tight…. Ah, fuck!" He begins going a little faster but then steadies his pace.

"Lorenzo… Fuck me harder! Please!" I beg like my life depends on him pounding into me.

He rams inside me and continues to slam persistently, giving me pleasure with each thrust, and it's the sweetest assault on my pussy I've ever felt.

Damn, it's been so long since I've been intimate with someone.

Damn, it's never been like this before.

"Lorenzo! I'm coming again! Oh my God!" I release onto him as he continues pounding into me. It's the exact definition of fireworks exploding into the night sky on the Fourth of July. It's the eruption of Mount Vesuvius, finally letting go after nearly a hundred years.

Seconds later, he's finally letting go as well.

Once we're done, he falls beside me and wraps his big strong arms around mine. This feels almost as good as what he just did to me.

Almost.

I feel him taking in a deep, relaxed breath. "That was completely amazing."

"It was," I say, snuggling into him.

He places a kiss on the top of my head. "Good night, sweetheart."

"Good night, love."

He squeezes me tighter into his chest, and I know for damn sure that I'm not going to be humping any walls at my apartment tonight because there's no way I'm going home. I'm going to stay right here, lying right beside him for the rest of the night.

I want to stay like this for the rest of my life.

Chapter Eighteen

CARISSA

I wake up to the feel of sweet kisses on my cheek. I smile before opening my eyes, quickly remembering last night.

"Good morning, beautiful," Lorenzo whispers into my ear.

"Good morning, love," I reply.

His arms wrap around me just like they had the night before, and I relish in the feel of being in his embrace.

It feels so good to be close to him like this. To feel wanted, sexy, loved...

I know I've fallen for him, but how does he feel about me? I know he likes me, obviously. But is there more from his part?

Maybe it's too soon.

It's definitely too soon.

I'm the crazy one who falls head over heels in love with a guy after only knowing him for a couple of weeks...

"You hungry, beautiful?" He places another kiss on my cheek and rubs my belly.

I giggle because he is being gentle, and it tickles. "I am actually."

He chuckles too. "I figured. Your belly is telling me you are."

I shrug. "You took a lot out of me last night."

He squeezes me tighter. "So did you. How about I get up and make us some breakfast and then we can pick up right back where we left off last night? Maybe we can soak in the tub and you'll let me massage you in there."

"That sounds amazing," I respond, closing my eyes and imagining the two of us getting naughty in the bathtub. I feel a pool beginning to form between my thighs. Would it be wrong of me to ask him to eat me for breakfast instead?

My stomach growls again and he chuckles once more, kissing the top of my head. "And that's my cue. Let me go whip something up real quick. You stay right here, naked and beautiful." He runs a hand over my body, squeezes my tit, and grips my ass.

"Oh my God, Lorenzo…" I lean my head back into him.

He inserts two fingers into my cunt, then massages and makes little circles, making me want to explode already.

"Damn, look at you, sweetheart. Dripping wet and ready to go."

"Lorenzo, don't stop…" I beg.

He kisses my neck, increasing his speed. "I'm not planning on it, baby. I'm going to make you feel good all day today. My mission is to make you feel amazing. We're going to be naked in bed all day. Fuck, you feel so good… Your pussy is so soft."

I feel my release building up, and right as I'm about to let go, he slips his hard cock into my pussy from behind, making my orgasm that much more intense.

"Fuck! Lorenzo!" I grip onto his sheets, enjoying the sensation of it once more.

"Come, baby! Come for me!"

A rushing wave of pleasure leaks out of me and coats him as he continues thrusting into me.

"You're a beast," I say, as he flips me around. "Why didn't you finish too?" I place a kiss on his lips.

He smiles. "I told you. Today is all about you and making you feel amazing. I'm planning on coming later. Much later."

Pulling away, he rises from the bed and leaves me to watch him walking to grab his sweats from the night before. He puts them on, and the way they hang on his hips is completely immaculate and flawless. He's fucking amazing in every way possible.

He turns around and faces me with a smile. "Damn, babe."

"What?" I smile, pulling up the sheet to cover myself. I can't believe how open he makes me feel that I was just lying here naked like we've been at this for years. Then again, we pretty much let ourselves go without a second thought last night.

"Just looking at you like that... your hair a mess, hanging down around your face, your pink-flushed 'just orgasmed' cheeks, your breasts sticking out from the top of the sheets, and me knowing that you're completely naked under there and I had you time and time again? Perfection. You're pure perfection."

I giggle and adjust my hair, not really giving a care in the world about it since hearing how he feels about it—me. "That's funny, because I feel the same way about you," I say.

He comes up to the bed and leans down to kiss me once more. "Let me go make us something. I'll be back in a little while and serve you in bed."

I smile as he pulls back and heads out the door.

He wants to serve me breakfast in bed? I don't think anyone has ever done that for me before. Not a lover anyway. Sure, I've been brought food when I was too sick to get out of bed, but not in a sexual way like he's indicating.

I let the covers fall off me and move to where he was lying on the bed. I flip over to my belly and close my eyes, breathing in deeply. I can smell his masculine scent, and it sends shivers down my spine. It reminds me of the way he felt when he was on top of me.

When I open my eyes, I take notice of his nightstand and the photograph on it. It's of a woman with long blonde hair and deep-blue eyes—just like Gianna's. I instantly realize who it is. It's his wife.

Or late wife.

She was beautiful, and I frown, thinking once again how hard it must have been on Lorenzo to lose her.

But as I continue looking at the picture, something about her gives me the feeling of déjà vu. Something about her looks so damn familiar. Where have I seen her before?

Something is not sitting right with me.

I can't put my finger on it, but I know for a fact I've seen her before. As a matter of fact, I remember that when I first saw Lorenzo leaving the bar the first night, I thought I had seen him somewhere else too. But where?

Then it hits me. Flashes from five years ago dart to the front of my mind and tears well in my eyes.

I need to get out of here. I need to leave and quickly. I can't do this anymore.

I hop out of bed and fumble through my clothes, getting dressed.

This was a mistake. I should have never given in and started seeing Lorenzo. I should have stayed in my little hole, curled up to myself.

At least this way I'm taking my heart back off the table for a gamble. I gave him the power to hurt me, even if he doesn't know it.

Leaving now is going to destroy me inside, but what can I do? I can't stay. I sure as shit can't stay. I need to go.

Fuck. My jeans and boots. They're in the kitchen. I can't even sneak out through the back.

Whatever. He's going to know I'm gone sooner or later.

I'll just tell him I had an emergency or something. I don't know. I just know I have to leave.

I race to the kitchen and see Lorenzo whipping up batter and frying some bacon on the stove. The smell wafts into my nose for the first time, and it smells amazing.

But I can't stay. I need to leave.

He flips around and sees me grabbing my jeans from one of the dining room chairs. "Hey, you got dressed? I was going to come in and—"

"Something came up," I say, cutting him off because it's pointless to let him talk when I already know what he's going to say, and it'll just break my heart. "I have to go... the hospital." I immediately hate myself for using that as my excuse, but it's the first thing that comes to my mind.

I button my jeans and throw on my boots. It's a good thing these are just slip-ons.

"You're leaving? Hey, what's wrong? Your eyes are all red." He places the bowl with the batter onto the counter and walks toward me.

But he never reaches me because I back up. "I'm sorry... I'm fine. I have to go."

I turn around and march toward the front door. My heart is pounding at a million miles per minute, but at the same time, with each step I take, it's breaking into a million pieces.

I don't want to leave. It's the last thing I want to do. I want to stay here with him and pretend like I don't remember five years ago.

But now I can't unremember it. I can't just forget about it. I know I can't do this. It's going to kill me to get over him when I had just fallen in love with him.

Tears crash down my cheeks as I hear his steps behind me. I grab my coat off the couch and quickly throw it on. I don't even care if it's on right.

"Carissa, wait... What's wrong?"

I quickly unlock the door, open it, and without saying a single word to him, I head to my car.

Chapter Nineteen

LORENZO

"Daddy! Nonna and I are going to make cookies!" Gianna throws herself into my lap, almost making me drop the bottle of beer in my hands.

"That's nice, princess. That sounds like so much fun."

Her eyes light up, and her smile widens. "Yes! It's going to be fun. We're going to decorate them with icing and sprinkles." She takes a breath and hops off my lap. "Hi, Uncle Maxy." She waves at my brother who is sitting across from me and then plops herself onto his lap.

"Hi, pretty girl," he says, smiling at her, then takes a pull from his beer.

"Gia! Come, sweetheart. It's time!" my mother calls from the kitchen.

"Oh, boy! I have to go now! Bye, Daddy! Bye, Uncle Maxy!"

She races out of the living room before either of us has a chance to say good-bye.

My brother throws me a glance. "She's full of excitement. She's something special, that one." He chuckles.

"Yeah, she is," I say, expressionless, then take another swig.

Max raises an eyebrow. "So you wanna tell me what's been eating at you, man?"

"Huh?"

He smirks, unpleased. "Don't *huh* me, man. What's been going on with you? You've been a bump on a log all freaking day."

I shrug.

"Come on, Enz. Don't make me come over there and beat it out of you."

His threat is the first thing that makes me chuckle all damn day, but I'm not amused at all. I'm feeling pretty miserable and down.

"Yeah, like that would ever happen," I reply. Shrugging again, I say, "Remember how I said there was something I would be telling you?"

Maybe now's a good a time as ever to let him know about Carissa. Except now, there's a sad ending.

Because she won't pick up or return any of my calls.

Because she won't text me back.

Because she's been ignoring me ever since she took off yesterday morning.

Damn, what did I do wrong? One minute, we were both having a great time, enjoying one another—and I know for a fact she was enjoying it—and the next, she can't leave my house fast enough.

I'm going to regret telling him the first part because I know he's going to pick on me. But maybe, just maybe, when he hears the rest of it, he'll end up feeling sorry for my pathetic ass. Maybe.

Max has never really taken it easy on me, so I guess we'll see.

He nods.

"That chick you thought I was staring at?"

"The one with the amazing lips and eyes from the bar that night?"

I chuckle to myself. "Yeah, her."

His eyes widen, and I definitely have his full attention.

"Well, I kept bumping into her... so much so, I saved her one night from her ass of an ex."

He chuckles. "Ha, no shit?"

"Yeah. Anyway, we got to talking, and we ended up seeing one another for a bit."

He almost chokes on his beer. "You're joking, right?"

"Nah, man. I'm serious."

"And you never told me till now? You ass!"

I shrug. "Yeah, well, that's not all of it."

"Oh, so what's up? And why the hell are you so down about it? That chick was gorgeous. You should be on cloud nine right now."

I let out a deep sigh. "Well, I was... up until yesterday."

He furrows his brows.

Do I tell him all about our little evening together?

Hmm, maybe I'll skip the juicy parts. Those are only for me... and my memory now because she's gone.

Damn, she's gone. The realization hits me hard. I really thought things were going so well. I really thought things were progressing and going somewhere.

I thought she could be the one.

The one to save me from my misery.

The one to help me understand that life doesn't have to end when a loved one dies.

It's hard to keep holding on to someone who is no longer there.

"Bro, I couldn't even tell you if I wanted to. One minute everything is going so well, and the next, she's in a rush to leave. I don't know what I did or didn't do to make her so upset."

He places a hand underneath his chin. "Well, are you sure she's upset with you? If you're saying you have no idea why, then maybe she's not."

I shake my head. "She's never ghosted me before. She won't answer or return any of my calls, and she won't text me back. I don't know what to do." I bring my head down into my hands and drive my fingers through my hair.

"Something doesn't sound right. Have you tried going to see her?" he asks.

I lift my head back up and look over at him. "I mean, should I? Yeah, I've thought about it, but if she's ignoring me, should I really be going to her house? I don't know, man. Maybe I should just forget it. Maybe this is what I get for trying to move forward with my life. I'm not meant to be happy again. My time came and went when Sylvia passed." I bring my head back down into my hands. I feel tears forming behind my eyes. How can my life be this way?

"Dude, are you kidding me? Hey, look at me, Enz."

I move my head back up slowly and meet his gaze. I know he sees my watery eyes, but I don't know how long I'll be able to hold the tears at bay.

"Do you honestly think you're supposed to spend the rest of your life alone because Sylvia passed away, way too soon?"

I shrug my shoulders. I want to look away, but Max's stare won't let me go.

He shakes his head. "No, Lorenzo. That's not how it's supposed to go. This is not how your story ends. You're entitled to be happy and find happiness... for you and Gianna. Don't you think she deserves a mother in her life? Sure, she's got Mom and Marianna as mother figures, but I can guarantee you, she's missing a mom, you know?"

"I get that, but what am I supposed to do? Shit didn't work out, and honestly, it's probably better this way." I wipe at my eyes before tears fall onto my cheeks. "It wouldn't be fair to Sylvia for me to just move on."

"Weren't you the one who said it would be moving forward, not moving on? You're always going to love Sylvia, no matter what. She was your wife. She was everything to you."

He's right, but now I don't want to hear any more. I stand.

"Nope, sit your ass back down. I'm not finished. We're going to talk about this."

I let out a deep breath and sit back down, across from him on the opposite couch.

"Look, bro. What about what's fair to you, Enz? What about your happiness? Don't you think Sylvia would want you to be happy and live a happy life above anything else? You falling in love and being with someone who makes you happy would be the thing your wife would want the most—even if she's no longer here. Trust me, I knew Sylvia. We were close; you know that. I can tell you she loved you so freaking much. She would absolutely want you and Gianna to be happy."

There's no doubt in my mind he's one hundred and fifty percent right. He knew Sylvia almost better than I knew her myself. They had a great brother-in-law–sister-in-law bond, and he's right. Of course she'd want me to be happy.

I shake my head back and forth. "Yeah, I know. She would want that. But what do I do now? Carissa wants nothing to do with me."

"Enz, do you love her?"

I shrug.

Max chuckles for only a second before saying, "Nope. That's not going to work. You either do or you don't. There's no in between. If you're not there yet, then you don't right now, but if you are, it's a yes."

I don't say anything. I just stare at my brother dumb-foundedly, not knowing how to answer.

He scratches his head and drains the rest of his beer. "I'm going to ask you one last time, and you're going to give me a straight answer… or else."

I furrow my brows. "Or else what? Since when do you threaten me?"

"Since I know what's best for you, big bro."

I smirk at him, shaking my head.

"Enz?"

"Yeah?"

"Lorenzo?"

I grimace. "Yes, Massimo?"

"Lorenzo Trevano?"

I let out an annoyed breath. "Oh my God, dude! What?!"

He laughs. "Just wanted to make sure I have your attention."

"Yeah, yeah. You got it. Now, what the hell do you want?"

"Do you love Carissa? Yes or no?"

I take a moment to ponder his question. By no means is it a simple one, but the answer is so obvious. I've known it for a while.

"I do." I give him my most serious expression, letting him know I'm sure of my decision.

He nods. "I knew it. I could tell by the way you were talking about her. I sensed it. Otherwise, I wouldn't have even asked you in the first place, but I wanted you to realize it yourself."

"Yeah, man. I knew. *I know.* But it's too late. She won't talk to me."

He adjusts his collar. "It's never too late when you love someone. It's always worth fighting for them. Till the very end. Like you fought for Sylvia for so long. Until she couldn't hold on any longer."

I take a deep breath. His words ring so much truth. I had fought for Sylvia until she couldn't hold on any longer. I stayed with her and loved her until the very end. I prayed and prayed, hoping for a miracle that never came. In the end, I had to let her go. She was suffering and in pain, so in a way, her passing brings a sense of peace. As much as it killed me to let her go and move forward, it's good to know she's no longer suffering and hurting like she was before.

"Okay, so now what?" I ask.

A smile pulls across his face from ear to ear. "Now, you're going to do exactly as I tell you, and win her over the old-fashioned way."

"The old-fashioned way?"

"That's right. Now, pay attention."

Chapter Twenty

CARISSA

I swing my legs over the bed and insert my feet into the pink plush slippers I received from Emy for Christmas. They're soft and warm and perfect for this chilly day.

As I rise from my bed, I grab the polka dotted robe I got from Daniela and wrap myself around in it. This, too, is perfect for the chill in the air. I think today is supposed to hit the low twenties. Snow is a definite possibility.

I head out of the bedroom and walk into the bathroom. I almost scare myself when I take in my reflection in the mirror above the sink. My hair is tangled, my eyes are red and puffy, and right underneath them, dark heavy luggage has aged me ten years. Jesus. I look like a damn monster.

After using the bathroom, I head toward the kitchen. I desperately need some coffee. It was a long night of tossing and turning and not being able to relax, hence why I look the way I feel this morning.

I go grab a mug from the cabinet to make myself a double shot of coffee and almost drop it at the sound of the doorbell ringing.

My eyes dart to the time on the microwave: six forty-five. Who the hell wants to die, ringing my bell before seven in the morning? I grunt, place the mug onto the counter, and head to the intercom.

I push the white button to talk. "Who is it?"

"*Who is it?* Who are you expecting?! Open up, wench! I'm freezing!"

Shit. Is it Tuesday already? I've lost track of the days.

I press the red button on the intercom to unlock the building. Two minutes later, there's knocking on my door.

"Woman! You left me outside long enough. Did you want frozen coffee? You could've told me. I would've picked that up instead at Dunkin'." Shannon walks in with a bag of food and a tray of coffee. She makes her way to the kitchen and places it onto the table.

I totally forgot about our Tuesday morning ritual because I didn't even remember it was Tuesday.

She takes out bagels and cream cheese from the brown paper bag, and as she does, she gives me a once-over.

She raises an eyebrow and stops unbagging. "Damn, Cariss… You look like you got hit by a truck." She removes her coat and places it behind her chair.

"I might as well have," I say, slipping into one of the chairs at the table.

"Did you sleep at all? You forgot I was coming over, didn't you?"

I shrug. "Barely."

"Good thing I picked up breakfast this morning or you'd starve me. Here. You need this." She hands me a cup of coffee.

"Thanks."

She sits on one of the chairs next to me and grabs a bagel from the six she brought. She reaches into the bag and picks out a plastic knife and then starts spreading the cream cheese.

"You should probably get some food in your system too," she says as she takes a sip of her coffee.

I finally lift my eyes to look at her. "I'm not really hungry."

Shannon shakes her head and takes a bite of her bagel. "I knew you were going to say that. You wanna tell me what's up? Did you run into Steve again?" She puts her bagel onto her plate and dusts her hands. "Fuck, you did, didn't you?" She pulls out her cell phone from her pocket. "Let me call Emerson. Did you tell Lorenzo?"

I shake my head fiercely as I place my cup down. I wave my hands at her. "No, stop. I didn't run into Steve. I haven't seen him since that night."

Since that night when Lorenzo saved me.

Damn, I miss him so much. It's been two days—or is it three now—and not talking to him or seeing him is making me crazy. It's been so hard not to answer his calls or respond to any of his text messages. My fingers get itchy and want to reply.

But I can't. I know I can't. I know I have to stay away and let go of him.

Even if it is breaking my heart.

I never thought I'd feel this way about him when we first met. I can't believe how easily I fell for him.

He made it so easy to love him.

He made it so easy to *fall in love* with him.

I reach out and touch her hand. "Put your phone down, Shannon."

She looks at me, unsure of what to do. "You're scaring me, Carissa. Are you feeling all right? Are you sick?"

Yeah, I'm sick. I'm suffering of a broken heart. "No, I'm not sick. Lorenzo and I... we just didn't—"

Her eyes widen just a little bit. "You broke up with him?"

It's funny to me how she knows I'm the one who ended it. Of course I did. I'm Carissa Rodgers, and I'm not capable of keeping a relationship.

I get scared.

I run away.

It's what I do, and I know it.

When I don't answer her, she takes a sip from her coffee and then responds. "Jesus, Cariss. Why would you do that? He was such a good guy… wasn't he?"

The best.

"I don't know." I shrug and copy her by drinking some coffee. The piping-hot liquid is exactly what I need right now, and it tastes so good. She always goes to my favorite bakery in town to get me this coffee. Their bagels are amazing too. By now, I would have already scarfed down two. And their muffins and other baked treats? They're to die for.

"You don't know? Did he do something to piss you off? Or you just don't like him anymore?"

Like him? That's not even a question. I love Lorenzo, but she doesn't know that. And I'm trying desperately to get over him. That's why I'm ducking his calls.

She takes another bite of her bagel, and now my stomach is growling, but I don't think I'm hungry. I think I'm feeling sick over the end of my time with Lorenzo.

I shake my head. "He didn't do anything."

She looks at me with a scowl. "So you pushed him away just because you felt like it? You got scared and needed a way out?"

I shrug. "Something like that."

I don't dare tell her about what I saw. Not yet anyway.

"Carissa!" she scolds.

"What?"

"You don't push people away because you chicken out, especially when they're good to you. What's wrong with you? Don't you want to move on from the past and enjoy your life?"

Easy for her to say. Shannon's got an amazing man. Fiancé. Whatever.

When I don't respond, she throws her hands onto the

table and rises from her seat. She grabs her coat and puts it on. "Forget this."

"You're leaving?" I ask, watching her put her arms through the sleeves.

She finally meets my gaze and throws her purse over her shoulder. "Yes, I'm leaving. You want to be miserable, fine. Be miserable. I'm not going to sit here and watch you wallow in your own misery three years after Steve left you. I'm done feeling sorry for you and letting you waste your life on a piece of shit who didn't deserve you. He never did. Now you wanna go and throw away something good you had with Lorenzo? Whatever, that's on you. I'm not sitting here anymore. I'm—"

"He was Sylvia's husband!" I finally blurt. I can't take her blaming all of this on me. It's not completely my fault for sending him away. I have my reasons.

And the look on her face right now tells me I made the right choice by walking away.

Chapter Twenty-One

LORENZO

I haven't bothered going back home. I mean, what's even the point? Gianna loves staying at Nonna's house. She hasn't wanted to leave; she's having too much fun with my parents and her aunt and uncle. I can't blame her. She's the only kid, so they spoil her to no end.

Sure, I could leave her here and return home, maybe even get back to the gym and work out, but I haven't been in the mood lately. Ever since everything happened with Carissa, I haven't felt like doing much of anything, and going home would be a definite reminder of the night we spent together.

The way she felt in my arms.

The way she smelled like lavender.

The way she tasted like candy canes and heaven.

Fuck, I miss her. I wish she'd answer my calls.

I pull out my cell phone and look through it, checking to see if I missed a text from her or anything.

I've been the only one doing any texting here, and these are only the ones I've sent since last night. There are more from the previous couple of days. I'm going to reread them to see if I could have better said anything else.

Me: Hey, Carissa. How are you?

Me: I miss you.

Me: Carissa, are you there?

Me: I'm sorry.

I know it was a ton of messages to send someone back to back, but I'm wise enough to know that when I have something good, not to let it all go. Max told me to keep texting her, and I did. But I've got one last thing up my sleeve.

Me: Baby, I'm sorry. I don't know what I did or didn't do, but I'm truly sorry and miss the fuck out of you.

Me: Carissa, sweetheart, whatever upset you, let's talk about it, please.

"Hey, Enz. You ready? There's like fifteen minutes till midnight. Mom, Dad, and Mari are in the living room waiting so we can pop a bottle. You coming?"

I look up at my brother standing in the doorway of my old bedroom. Yeah, it's New Year's Eve, but I'm so miserable, I don't want to celebrate. What good is the new year going to be if I have to start it like this?

"Is Gianna still asleep?" I ask, putting my phone next to me on the bed.

He nods, leaning against the doorframe. "Yeah, she's on Mom and Dad's bed, knocked out. Poor thing tried so desperately to wait till midnight."

I nod. "Okay, I'll be right there."

Max pushes off the doorframe and knocks on his lap. "Okay, bro. I'll be out there waiting for you."

He walks away, and I rise from the bed. Heading down the hallway toward the kitchen, I stop when I pass my parents' bedroom. I sneak in and see my princess lying there, fast asleep. The rise and fall of her chest lets me know she's out for the night. I push some hair out of her face and place a kiss on her cheek. "Happy New Year, sweetheart. Daddy loves you so much."

Gianna stirs and opens her eyes. Crap, I didn't mean to wake her.

"Hi, Daddy."

A smile pulls at the corners of my lips. No matter what I'm going through, this little girl can always put a smile on my face. I'm so grateful for her.

As I go to pick her up off the bed, her next words stop me dead in my tracks.

"Daddy, why does the pretty lady not talk to you anymore?"

I swallow hard. "Pretty lady?"

She nods and turns onto her back. "Yeah, your friend. She had pretty red lipstick. I want to wear lipstick too."

I don't know how to answer her. How does she even know? Maybe she overheard me talking to Max. I'm thankful when she quickly changes the subject on her own.

"Daddy, is it time?"

I smile. "Yes, princess. It's time. Come on, let's go."

I pick her up, and she lays her head on my chest. Maybe this isn't so bad. Maybe Carissa not being in my life is okay. All I need is my daughter.

I shake my head. I'm fucked. Yeah, all I do need is my daughter, but I sure as hell wouldn't mind having Carissa in my life too. I miss her so fucking much.

I make my way out of the bedroom with Gianna in my arms and walk into the living room. My brother is sitting on the recliner, my parents are cuddled up together on one of the couches, and my sister is texting on her phone on an opposite one.

How crazy life is. My brother is single, no worries, no troubles, no problems. My parents, the epitome of what a true couple is supposed to look like, are happy and in love after almost forty years of marriage. My sister and her husband, Jordan, are probably on the verge of divorce.

And then there's me... complicated as fuck. I don't even know where I fall. Whatever I had with Carissa is gone now.

"Gianna, you woke up, princess?" my father asks. He and my mom smile at her.

She's got her thumb in her mouth, but she nods softly with her head against my chest.

"Bring her here," my mother says.

I walk over to where she's sitting and place Gianna in her arms. My daughter easily latches on to my mom.

"You made it just in time to bring in the new year, princess," she says to Gianna and kisses her head.

"Everything good, Enzo?" my father asks me. He's always called me Enzo. I don't particularly like it, but it is what it is. He makes the rules around here, and I quickly learned growing up that you don't test the boss.

"Yeah, sorry. I had to go through some stuff with Ryker from the gym."

My mom nods. "All good, honey. You want to get the champagne? We'll need your strength to pop it open." She's so sweet. My dad usually pops the bottles open, but tonight, they're noticing something is up with me. They've known it since everything happened. I know they're trying to get my mind off things, even if they don't really know what's going on.

I leave the living room, walk into the kitchen, and find the bottle of champagne. I had already seen the glasses spread out on the coffee table in the living room, so I grab the bottle and make my way back.

"It's time," my brother announces as he switches the channel to ABC so we can catch the countdown at Times Square. Fifteen seconds to go.

Max points at the TV. "Here it is. Ten, nine..."

I think back to the messages I sent Carissa as the loud television and the excitement everyone else is feeling blasts through my ears.

> **Me: I don't know what happened and why all of a sudden you pulled away. I really thought you enjoyed everything we did, but if I went too far, I'm so sorry. I didn't mean to upset you or offend you or whatever the case may be. I don't know what it could be... Please tell me so I can correct it.**

"Eight, seven..."

> **Me: I really want to talk and fix this... you mean so much to me. Please answer me.**

"Six, five..."

> **Me: All I want to do is say I'm sorry and right things with you. The last thing I wanted was for you to go away and no longer even speak to me.**

"Four, three..."

> **Me: If you'd rather we be just friends, that's fine. It'll hurt to let you go, but I'm a grown ass man and I can handle it. I'd**

**rather you tell me you want that instead
of completely ignoring me. Please.**

"Two, one…"

I grip the bottle tightly in one hand and place my other hand on the edge of the cap, getting ready to pop it open.

"Happy New Year!"

Everyone stands and congratulates each other. The lid pops off and everyone cheers. Glasses are filled, toasts are said, and we all drink champagne. My mother handed Gianna a glass of sparkling apple cider to feel like she was part of the celebration as well. She's not a fan after only taking a sip.

After everyone calms down, I walk to the far end of the living room and take a seat on one of the couches.

I figure I need to send one last and final text. It's obvious I need to let her go. She doesn't want me, and she has no intention of even speaking to me anymore.

I take a deep breath and type my last message to her before I take my brother's plan on what I should do into consideration. I haven't done what he told me to do yet because I don't know how she will react, but maybe I need to. It'll be the last thing to try, and maybe it will get her to talk to me once more. She would have to thank me at least, right? Or maybe she'll trash everything and hate me even more. Time would tell, but it's my last option.

> *Me: Carissa, I'm sorry. I don't want to make things worse by continuing to text you when you obviously don't want to talk to me anymore. Hell, you probably already blocked my number, and I can't say I blame you. I know I'm persistent, but when I want something I fight for it. It's in my nature, and*

I can't help it. But I'm sorry. I wish you all the best, and in case you do ever want to talk, I'm here. Happy New Year. ~Lorenzo.

Chapter Twenty-Two

CARISSA

I can't believe it's already the new year. Every time I think back to the past year and everything that happened, especially the last two months, it blows my mind how much my life changed. Of course, I wish things could be different now, but still, I'm proud of how far I've come.

Yet, I'm devastated. I'm so torn by the last couple of days. I really thought something good was coming out of it. I was convinced and I let myself fall, then landed flat on my face. It sucks, but as soon as I told Shannon who Lorenzo was, she didn't fault me for pulling away. In fact, she understood my reasoning, to some point.

Now there's a new bouquet of flowers and box of candies waiting for me every day, making it harder to forget about him. I thought by not answering his calls or text messages—God, has it been hard not to talk to him—it would make him understand, but no. He went one step further and has been sending me flowers.

It's January sixth, the first Wednesday after the new year, and he's still not showing an end in sight.

"Hey, girl." Daniela walks into the break room and plops onto the seat next to mine.

I lift my gaze. "Hey, Dani."

"Man, today's been a long-ass day. I can't wait to get home and kick my feet up on the couch."

I nod. "Yeah, I'm not planning on doing much once I leave here either."

She sips her Diet Coke through a straw. "Any more word from Guns?"

Guns... I haven't heard him being referred to that in a long time. Immediately, thoughts of his big arms wrapped tightly around me cloud my brain. Damn... I miss him—and them—so much.

I swallow thickly and take a deep breath. "He stopped texting, but he's been sending me flowers and candy every day since the first."

Her eyes widen. "Oh my God, girl! He's so sweet. I can't believe you let him go. I get why and all, but don't you think enough time has passed since then?"

I shrug. "Maybe. But it's not something I can take a chance on. I'm checking out before my feelings are too far gone."

"Aren't you and your feelings already too far gone? I mean, you love him, right? Still?" She dips her hand inside the bag of Doritos and stuffs the one she grabbed into her mouth.

"I don't even know anymore." I look down because I can't stand talking about Lorenzo and everything else that could have been, what I've thrown away.

She's about to say something more, but I really need to take this conversation a different direction.

I clear my throat. "So, how's your family?"

She smirks but doesn't push. This is one of the reasons why we're friends. "They're good. They were driving me crazy with the holidays, so I'm glad that's over with. Now I can focus on work, and they can mind their own damn business."

I chuckle. "Their own business about what?"

She shrugs. "Everything. Because I live alone, my mother is always on my ass. She wants to make sure I'm taken care of, but I keep telling her I can take very well care of my damn self."

I smile. "She's your mom. It's what she's supposed to do." I instantly miss my mom and the way she used to be just like that with me and Shannon. It's been so long since she's been gone.

"Maybe, girl. But it's both a blessing and a curse to live so close to my parents." She takes another sip of her drink.

I smirk. "My older sister is enough to drive me crazy…"

Daniela laughs. "Yeah, I remember you saying she does all the time. But I guess that's with any older siblings."

I smile and rise from my seat. "I'm sure."

She frowns. "Ugh! Please don't tell me it's time to get back already."

"Unfortunately, there's about three minutes left. I figured I'd get started. Maybe I can cut out three minutes early."

She laughs. "Three minutes is definitely worth it."

"Ain't that the truth." I walk out of the breakroom and finish the rest of my shift.

***

It's Friday, and I couldn't have picked a better day to take off from work. Okay, so I'm not really sick, but lately sleeping has been shit for me. I've been spending hours tossing and turning in bed at night for the past week or so. I'm pretty sure this has nothing to do with Lorenzo at all. It's been long enough, hasn't it?

Probably not, and truthfully, it's probably all about him.

He's always on my mind. There's no way I could have already forgotten about him if I tried harder. Plus, he's still sending me flowers every day. My house is starting to look like a florist's shop.

I exhale heavily just as the doorbell rings. Great, that must be today's delivery. I wonder if it will be red roses or white. Maybe it'll be pink orchids again. Damn, where the hell am I going to put another bouquet of flowers?

I push the button to talk and say, "Just bring them up," and I push the other button to unlock the building.

Minutes later, four raps on my door come hard and fast.

"I'm coming, hang on," I announce.

I pull open the door and see the smiling faces of Emerson and Shannon holding a huge bouquet of pink-and-white orchids. Ah, so these are today's.

"What are you two doing here?" I ask as Shannon shoves the flowers my way.

"We came to pick you up, and the delivery guy was walking up to your door."

"He was kind of hot," Emy says as she and Shannon nod at one another.

They make their way past me and park their asses on my living room couches.

"Pick me up?" I ask, placing the gorgeous flowers on my table. Orchids are my favorite. I had only told Lorenzo once, and he clearly never forgot.

I walk to where the girls are. I wasn't planning on going anywhere tonight.

Emy taps her nails on the arm of the couch. "Yeah, we thought it would be best if we got you out of the house for a bit. Plus, it's Friday night."

I lean against the wall closest to the door. "I was actually planning on staying in tonight and getting some re—"

"You're not reading tonight," Shannon says, interrupting me.

I smirk. "How did you know I was even going to say that?"

"Because that's all you ever wanna do, li'l sis. Now, go throw on some clothes and let's go."

I throw Emy a glance, but she's busy texting someone on her phone.

I turn my attention back toward Shannon. I don't really want to go, but I know better than to fight with them right now. "Where are we going?"

Shannon smiles from ear to ear. "To forget all about our troubles. We're going drinking."

"And don't tell us you don't really drink because we saw you on Christmas and New Year's Eve," Emy says, not bothering to even look up from her phone.

She's right though. Lately, I have enjoyed drinking a lot more.

"Okay, let me go get changed," I say, making my way toward my bedroom.

"Good, girl!" Emy and Shannon respond in unison in a singsong voice.

I better not regret agreeing to this.

We arrive at the bar almost forty-five minutes later, and as I walk in, my eyes land on Lorenzo Trevano, and I freeze in place.

Chapter Twenty-Three

LORENZO

When I agreed to go out with Marianna and Max tonight, I didn't know I'd see her again. I thought we were just going out for drinks, and I wasn't thrilled. I wanted to stay in and rot.

My brother and sister begged me to go out for hours before I gave in and said fuck it. What else was I going to do on a Friday night? As miserable as I was, maybe it was for the best.

We've been sitting in Bottoms Up for the past twenty minutes without any excitement. We downed a few drinks. I've had more than Max or Mari, but I'm the one who needs alcohol the most. Maybe Mari does too. Jordan finally called her earlier today to tell her he'd be home tomorrow. He wouldn't tell her where he's been for the last few weeks, but I'm sure it's something they're going to have a talk about sooner or later. I know my sister is stressed out, and I can't blame her. I just hope this bastard doesn't break her heart anymore. I know she's hurting.

Fuck, I really wish she'd let me rearrange his face with my fists. The son of a bitch deserves it.

As I'm deep in my thoughts of how I'd love to make

Jordan pay for what he's doing to Marianna, something tells me to look at the entrance of the bar, and that's when I see her.

Carissa, dressed in a pink shirt and tight blue jeans, walks into the bar with her sister and best friend.

Our eyes lock, and my heart skips a beat. Damn, she still has the power to make me feel like I'm floating on a cloud, and I don't want to be brought back down. I want her to come up to me and let me place my lips on her until we're both floating away from the rest of the world.

And just like that, I'm reminded of how empty the last couple of days without her have been. Seeing her now after all we've been through is breaking my heart. Because I know she still probably hates me, but for what, I don't know. It's the part that's been driving me crazy.

"I have to go talk to her," I say, rising to my feet.

Marianna and Max nod, and as I look back at where Carissa is, she's turning around on her heels and getting ready to leave.

No! I can't let her leave without telling her how I feel in person. I need to talk to her. I need to pour my heart out to her and place all my cards on the table. I can't lose her.

I race to get to the door, fumbling over some chairs at nearby tables. Why the hell does it have to be so tight in here?

I excuse myself to the customers I get in the way of as I rush to get to the door before she has a chance to escape. This is my last chance to talk to her. The flowers had done nothing to get her to call me, no matter how many times I said "I'm sorry" in the notes.

It still drives me fucking crazy that I don't have the slightest idea as to why she walked away and never returned. I can't fucking understand it. I just wish she'd tell me why.

"Carissa!" I shout, stumbling over my own feet. Dammit, the last thing I need is to fall flat on my face.

She spins her head around once more to look at me but turns right back around and keeps trying to push her way through. Her sister, Shannon, and best friend, Emy, are trying to stop her from leaving. Good, maybe they're on my side.

Yeah, I really doubt that's the reason, but who knows.

"Carissa, wait," I say, finally reaching her. "Hey, look at me."

She finally turns back around, and my eyes lock with hers once more. God, she's so beautiful. I missed seeing her gorgeous face so much. It breaks my heart to know she couldn't wait to get away from me, but I need to put that aside and focus on what I need to say to her.

"Can we talk?" I ask, hoping she'll give me one last chance.

She looks hard at me, thinking it over, then turns toward Shannon and Emy, who both nod.

I flash a glance back at my brother and sister, and they're nodding at me too. Why does it feel like this was a setup?

"We're going to give you two some privacy. Come on, Em," Shannon says, pulling Emerson to the side.

"Carissa..." It comes out as barely a whisper. My eyes are ready to overflow with tears.

She puts up a hand before I can say anything further. "Before you apologize again, I want to thank you for all the beautiful flowers and candy you sent me. You didn't have to, but it was very sweet."

I shake my head to let her know it was nothing. Words don't manage to come out. If this is how she's going to let me know for sure she's done with me, done with us, I don't know how I'm going to take it.

But I'm sad. I'm so damn sad, my heart feels like it's breaking before her.

She looks around, and her eyes land on an empty table to her right. "Let's sit down so we can talk."

I nod and we walk over and take a seat. She places both of her hands on the table, and I so badly want to take them in mine.

But I won't.

Because then she'll probably get up and walk away, and it'll all be over before I have a chance to speak.

Carissa takes a deep breath and says, "I wasn't going to talk to you. I was going to keep my distance and hope you'd forget all about me."

How could I forget about her? Ever since I laid eyes on her, all I can think about is her. There's no way her ignoring me would make me forget about her, not in the span of a couple of days anyway.

I search her eyes, trying to figure out why the hell she'd want me to forget her, but I still don't understand any more than I did the first day. None of this makes any fucking sense.

"But why?" I ask. "I don't understand. I thought things were going really well that day."

The day I held you in my arms and made love to you over and over, and again the following morning... before you left.

The thought stings, and I wish I could push it away.

She closes her eyes, and when she opens them, it looks like she's about to cry too. "They were. They were going really well. I was the happiest I had ever been in so long."

"Me too." I reach out and take her hands in mine without thinking twice. I need her to feel how much I mean this. She jerks but doesn't pull away. Maybe it's a good thing.

"You're a great guy, Lorenzo. You saved me, and not just that night in the parking lot. You saved me from a life I thought I was destined to have. For that, I'm forever thankful."

"So why did you leave?" I search her pretty eyes once more. Nothing. No sign, no giving anything away.

She looks at Shannon and Emerson, and I follow her

gaze. The two of them are already downing their drinks. My brother and sister, sitting a few tables away from them, are doing the same.

"You know I work at the hospital, correct?" she asks, bringing my attention back to her.

I nod. "Of course I do. I remember that." I remember everything she's ever told me.

She licks her luscious lips, and even though this is not the time, I can't help but want to kiss them. I miss tasting them so badly.

"I'm no doctor or nurse. I'm in the billing department. But even so, we see what goes on, and we become familiar with certain faces and what they're going through. I remember Sylvia, so very clearly. As soon as I saw her picture, the memories flooded my mind. During one of my shifts, I happened to walk past her room when she called out to me. It was weak, but somehow, I heard it." She pauses for a moment and then continues. "When I walked in, the devastating look on her face was enough to burn into the back of my mind. Typically, we don't get involved or even remember patients. But Sylvia? Sylvia was something special. She reminded me of my mom and how she looked when she passed, so much so that I even told my sister and my best friend about her. Her big eyes and stringy blonde hair? It was just my mom so long ago, and unfortunately, we lost her too soon."

"Oh, Carissa," I say, but she stops me from continuing.

She takes a deep breath and then closes her eyes. "Lorenzo, I'm just going to out and say this because there is no easy way around it. I was there the day Sylvia passed. I was there when you cried your eyes out and lost her that day. I watched you tear yourself apart the moment she was gone, and it broke me. It tore at my heart. I was able to see how deeply you loved her and how much she meant to you."

I narrow my brows, unsure of where she's going with

this. "You were there that day... How does this relate to us? I don't understand."

She takes another deep breath. "That morning when you left me... *in your bed*," she whispers the last three words, and it brings shivers up my spine, thinking of her lying there with me. It was perfect. "I happened to turn over and see the picture of Sylvia on your nightstand. I realized I had seen her before, as I knew I had seen you before we met too. I couldn't remember from where, but then, in an instant, it hit me, and the memories came crashing into the front of my mind, and I freaked out. The memories of my mom and the day Sylvia passed all came rushing back. I had to go."

"But—"

"Lorenzo, I got scared. I can't fall in love with you, and even though I'd already fallen, I needed to get up and pull myself away. I couldn't do it."

I swallow thickly. "Carissa, listen. I was so afraid to fall in love at first too, but I did. I did it anyway. You made me fall in love again, and it was beautiful. Albeit scary because I had been turned off to dating women for so long after my wife passed. But then I met you, and you changed my whole perspective on love and life."

She rubs her thumb over my hand. "Lorenzo, don't you get it? I'm afraid to be with you because I saw how much you loved your wife. How can I ever compete with that? How can you ever love me the same way? I'm afraid you'll never be able to, and maybe that's okay, but I'm also afraid of being hurt. I remember how devastated you were the day you lost her. I also remember how it felt when I got my heart broken by Steve. It hurts. It fucking hurts like hell, and I don't want to go through it again. I can never compete with what you had with her."

A frown forms on my face. I'm torn she feels this way. Could I ever love her like I loved Sylvia? I do, but at the same time, it's different. Not in a bad way, just different. I'll always love my wife, but I love Carissa too. "Oh, Carissa. I do love you… so much. And I will always love Sylvia as well. I'd be lying if I said I didn't, and I don't want to lie to you. She was my wife and the mother to my daughter. She was my first love, my everything. But just because I'll always love her doesn't mean I won't love you or that I'll love you less. You have to understand it's not a competition."

"It's not. I know that, but I have to let this go. I'm sorry." She pulls her hands away from mine and rises from her seat.

I don't let her go. I grab her hand before she can get away, and it forces her to look back at me. "It's not a competition, and if you say you have to go, then I'm going to fight for you, fight for us."

She furrows her brows and sits back down. "What?"

"Carissa, I'm going to fight because I realize you're worth it. If I need to spend every day for the rest of my life showing you you're worth fighting for, then so be it, baby."

"Lorenzo—"

I shake my head. "Look, I'm sorry for the constant phone calls, texts, and blowing up your phone these past couple of weeks. I'm sorry for not giving up. I'm sorry for coming into your life if all you ever wanted was solace, without me bringing my crazy world into yours."

"No, please don't say that. I—"

"Please let me finish."

She nods.

"I'm not giving up, Carissa, and guess what? I'm not sorry for fighting for someone I care so deeply about, someone I love. Yes, I love you, and I don't care if I'm crazy or whatever anyone else thinks because it happened so fast. I truly fucking love you, and I'll be damned if I give up now. I'm a fighter, and fighters don't quit."

She nods again, closing her eyes as a tear falls onto her cheek. I reach out and wipe at it with my hand, and she leans into it. She opens her eyes again.

I smile at her and continue. "Let me tell you what else I'm not sorry about. I'm not sorry for placing my lips on you that night and tasting the sweet candy cane sugar on your luscious lips."

She blushes, but I'm going to keep going because it's now or never.

"I'm not sorry for taking you into my arms and holding you tight. I'm not sorry for spending a magical evening with you and bringing your body to life."

"Lorenzo…" she whispers, looking around with her cheeks all flushed.

I smile at her, but I need to finish the rest of what I have to tell her. "Most of all, the one important thing I don't regret and am one hundred and fifty fucking percent not sorry about is finding you and realizing what an amazing fucking woman you are. I'm not sorry you saved me from the depression and the sorrow of my miserable life. I died a long time ago when I lost my wife, but you, you brought me back to life, and even if you don't forgive me now or want to be with me, I'm thankful you saved me. You saved me and made me realize this is worth fighting for. *You* are worth fighting for. I'm a UFC fighter. I'm used to fighting for what I want and, now, fighting for *who* I want. And I want you. You're worth fighting for, and I'm not backing down. I want this, and I want you. You're worth it. We're both worth it, and we owe this to ourselves. Please, don't walk away from this. Please give us a chance. I love you."

Her expression turns serious as she considers my words. I can tell she's unsure, but as she rises from her seat, I can already feel my heart start to sink.

I poured my heart out to her, placed all my cards on the table, yet they weren't enough. She's walking away from me.

I hang my head down. Maybe this is a fight I'm just not going to win. Maybe this is the one time I need to throw in the towel and realize I'm not undefeated anymore.

"Lorenzo…"

I hear her voice calling out to me, but she's closer this time.

I lift my gaze from the ground and see her standing in front of me. She hasn't left. She's still here.

"Carissa, you're still here."

She moves in closer and places herself in between my legs. I reach out and put my hands on her waist. She smiles her pretty smile at me, and my heart melts. My stomach knots with anxiety at the anticipation of not knowing what she's going to say next.

She nods. "I'm still here, and I'm not going anywhere. I want to be in the ring and fight. I want to fight for this but not against you. I want to fight with you and be on your side. I'm willing to fight with you if you are too. I love you so much. I don't want to let go—lose this… lose you."

I am up on my feet the second those words leave her lips. I'm so happy she feels this way because it's all I've wanted. I lift her off her toes and kiss her as though my life depends on it.

Because it does.

She does.

As we kiss, I hear Marianna, Max, Shannon, Emerson, and now even Ryker cheering for us. When then hell did he get here?

I bring Carissa down but keep her in my embrace. The two of us chuckle as we watch our friends coming toward us with the owner of the bar, Gage, carrying bottles of champagne and flutes. Gage has always been pretty cool, and it looks like they were all in on this and we're gonna celebrate getting back together.

This is definitely something worth celebrating.

As our friends fill our glasses and raise a toast in our names, my heart feels full, and I'm finally at peace after so many years of loneliness and heartache.

I know this is going to be a lot of work. I know it's not going to be easy, but I'm ready. I'm ready for the challenge, and I'm willing to do what I need to do to show Carissa how much I'm in this for the long haul. I'm in this for life, willing to fight for us.

Afterword

THANK YOU
So much for reading *Fighting for Us*
Book 1 in the *Love is Worth Fighting For* Series!

Did you enjoy Lorenzo & Carissa's story as much as I loved
writing it?
Well, book 2, *Fighting for Her*, will be coming soon!
You can expect to see appearances from your favorite
characters introduced in book 1, including Ryker! *Fighting for
Her* will be his story!!!

For more information on the series, please visit
www.BellaEmy.com

Acknowledgments

THANK YOU

A huge thanks goes out to my ARC & beta readers!

Thank you to Tara L. Ames, Alyssa Drake, Shannyn Leah, and the rest of the holiday crew. This project was a blast to work on, and Lorenzo & Carissa are now one of my favorite couples.

To all of Bella's Heartbreakers — you guys are the best!!!

Thanks to all my family & friends…. I adore you all so much!

With much love,
❤ Bella

About the Author

Bella Emy is a *USA Today* Bestselling Author.

She loves all books, but her favorite genre to read, as well as write, is romance. Bella loves creating heartbreaking stories that will deeply touch her readers, but in the end, a good HEA is usually the turnout.

Whenever Bella is not typing away on her computer with a nice hot cup of coffee, she loves spending time with her family and friends. Her favorite places to go are the movies, the beach, or just on a good plain old road trip. Some of her must haves are coffee, chocolate, pizza, music, & movies.

Breaking Hearts One Story at a Time

❤ Bella Emy ❤
www.BellaEmy.com

Follow Bella now on the following platforms:

facebook.com/bellaemywrites
twitter.com/bellaemywrites
instagram.com/bellaemywrites
bookbub.com/authors/bella-emy
pinterest.com/bellaemybooks

Also by Bella Emy

Check out some more books by Bella Emy!

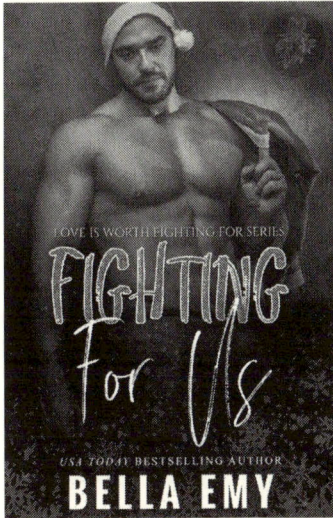

Lorenzo

I had it all.

A wonderful family with a loving wife who was my world and a beautiful baby girl.

I didn't need anything more to be rich in my eyes.

Then one day, everything changed and my world was ripped apart.

My wife, my everything, was taken from me, and I was left alone to raise our baby girl.

I was forced from late night sessions at the gym to changing diapers all by myself.

Thank God for the help I received from my parents and siblings or I would have been lost.

I accepted my fate of being alone with my baby girl and living life with just us two...

Until the day I met her, and she became everything worth fighting for.

Carissa

Life was so perfect.

A loving fiancé, wonderful friends and family, and a job I adored.

Until one day, my world was turned upside down and the man I loved threw the promise of forever down the drain and walked out of my life.

The day he walked out of my door, I knew that everything I had ever grown up to believe in was a lie.

Love is unconditional but love sure as hell doesn't last forever.

The vow to love me for the rest of our lives ended quickly as he pulled away from me, and buried himself in the arms of his ex.

I was left alone, cursing the male species and everyone who had found their happily ever after.

My sister and my best friend were the only ones there for me...

Until the day I met him, and he became everything worth fighting for.

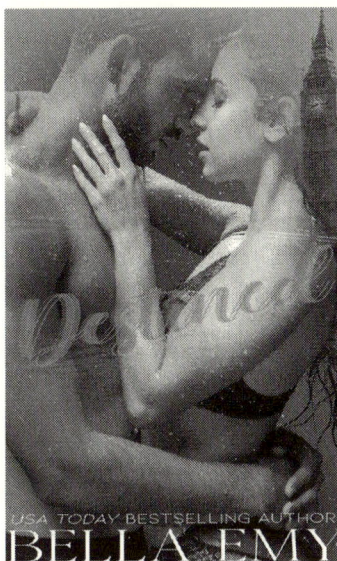

USA TODAY BESTSELLING AUTHOR

BELLA EMY

DESTINED

A brokenhearted physician falls for a lonely pianist across the globe on the anniversary of her late husband's death, failing to realize their lives have been entwined before they even met.

When a tragic accident steals my joy & my world on the magical holiday of Christmas, I'm left alone & have a hard time moving on.

Four years later, all I want on the anniversary of my husband's death is to spend this miserable holiday all alone.

When my best friend surprises me with a trip to London, it couldn't have come at a better time. I'm happy that I'll be getting exactly what I had wished for...

Until I run into the sexy pianist who has captured my attention from the first note I hear him play.

Getting to know him brings a smile to my face & a joy within my heart that I haven't felt in so long.

But something about him is so familiar... something I can't quite put my finger on until it blows up in my face.

When your heart has been shattered and torn into a million pieces, is it too late to find happiness once again?

Or will an unexpected encounter that was destined to occur bring on a happily ever after?

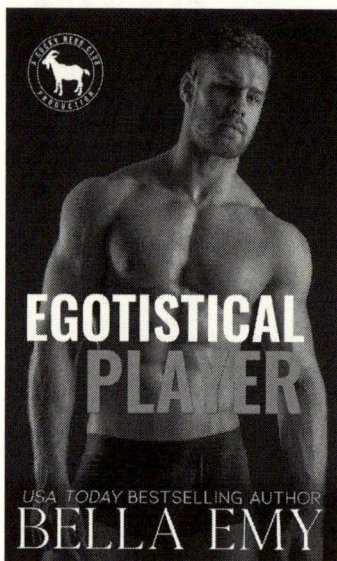

EGOTISTICAL PLAYER

Preston Scott.

Self-centered a$$hole.

Self-absorbed prick.

The king of supposed one-night stands, and my brother's best friend.

I hate him.

I loathe him.

I despise him.

I love him.

He's the man of my dreams and everything I know I should stay away from, but, oh, he's so irresistible.

The things he does to me, I can't keep my mind off of him.

But God, I need to keep my distance, yet I'm so drawn to him.

And then in an instant when my world is forever changed, Preston is the only one who I can turn to for comfort. He takes care of me, my mind, my soul, my heart, and my body.

But I know this can never last.

It's not in him to settle down, and he surely won't with his best friend's sister.

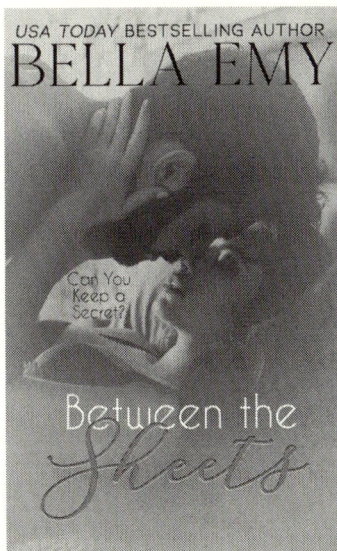

Derek, Derek, Oh, Derek!

BETWEEN THE SHEETS

A cocky, too-hot-for-his-own-good hunk and his twin sister's witty, sexy best friend set a plan in motion to hook up behind closed doors.

Can you keep a secret?

Ellie

I've been burned so many times, I lost count. I'm done with all men and their stupid games. All I want to do is find one guy who's willing to just give me pleasure, no strings attached. The one guy who'd be perfect is my best friend's twin brother, Derek. But that automatically makes him off limits.

Derek

I've wanted her from the first moment I saw her. But Lauren would never approve. Ellie is my sister's best friend. But damn, I can't get her out of my mind. No matter how many women I sleep with, she still haunts me. I can't get her out of my system.

When a plan is set into motion, what consequences will it bring?

Between the Sheets is intended for mature readers 18+ only.

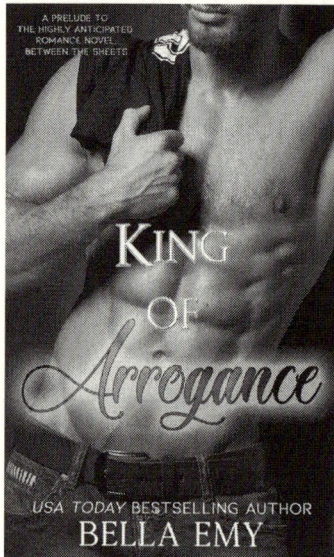

A PRELUDE TO
THE HIGHLY ANTICIPATED
ROMANCE NOVEL
BETWEEN THE SHEETS

KING
OF
Arrogance

USA TODAY BESTSELLING AUTHOR
BELLA EMY

KING OF ARROGANCE

Want a book to read in 5 mins that you don't really need to think about, but can get a few laughs from?

Well, Derek Mykels, the King of Arrogance, has got you covered!

He's arrogant, self-centered and all about himself.

She's the one he wants and he knows he'll have her.

It's just a matter of when and how he chooses to.

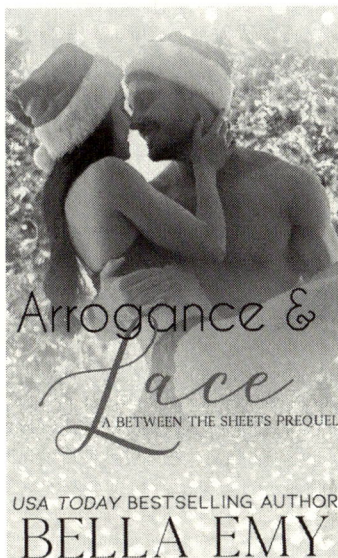

ARROGANCE & LACE: A BETWEEN THE SHEETS PREQUEL

One night of pure fun with the guys to get my mind off of her.

That's all it was supposed to be.

So what happens when three single dudes hit the bar looking to pick up chicks?

A whole lot of shenanigans and a whole bunch of laughs!

Join Derek, Danny, and Gage as they party one night right around the holidays. Will Mr. Derek Mykels get lucky and score, or will the girls put him in his place?

Arrogance and Lace is a *Between the Sheets* prequel short story written by *USA Today* Bestselling Author, Bella Emy. Find out what happens just days before Derek Mykels pursues his true love, Ellie Evers.

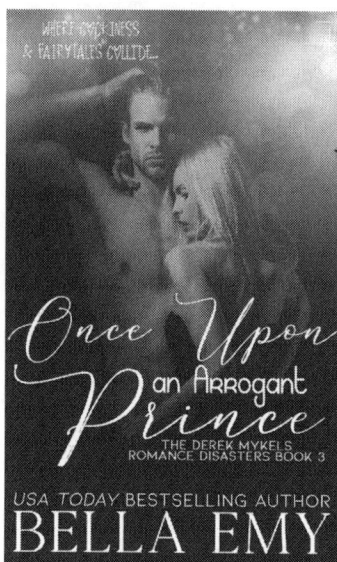

ONCE UPON AN ARROGANT PRINCE

Where cockiness & fairytales collide…

It's Christmas Eve and right now, the only place I want to be is home.

Except that I'm stuck at the freaking airport since Mother Nature had other plans in store: a monstrous blizzard with no end in sight.

There's no way I'll make it home in time for Christmas morning…

But when my eyes meet with the sexy stranger standing in front of me, things suddenly take a turn for the better.

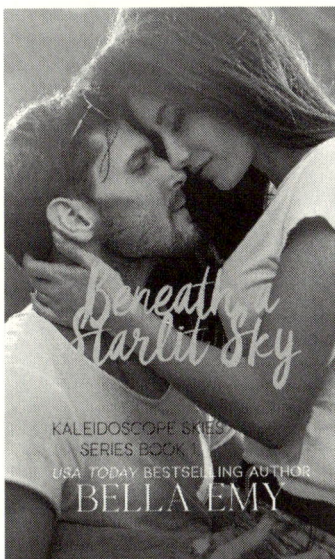

The Kaleidoscope Skies Series

BENEATH A STARLIT SKY

Fate brought them together...

Fate will tear them apart.

My first love.

The one I fell for so quickly.

The one who stole my heart and made me believe we had it all.

We did.

Till that fateful day when everything changed.

Beneath a Starlit Sky is a heart-wrenching, heartrending, tear-jerker! Not recommended for the weak at heart!

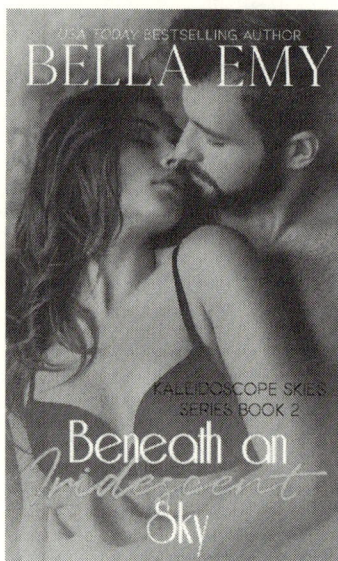

BENEATH AN IRIDESCENT SKY

I don't do relationships.

I haven't ever since the one man I thought was the one ended up shattering my poor, fragile

heart. I swore them off, steering clear of them like a bad case of the flu.

I went through my days, hopping in bed with one man and waking up next to another.

It was a foolproof plan meant to keep my heart in one piece, and so far, it had been working

for me just fine.

But on a trip with my best friend, Braelynn, down to New Orleans for the big Mardi Gras

celebration, I found more than I was hoping for. The whole point was to have fun and not worry

about a damn thing. A new-to-me city meant a whole new line up of the male species I was dying to try for the night.

Instead, I ran into a guy from so long ago who had never caught my eye before.

Until now.

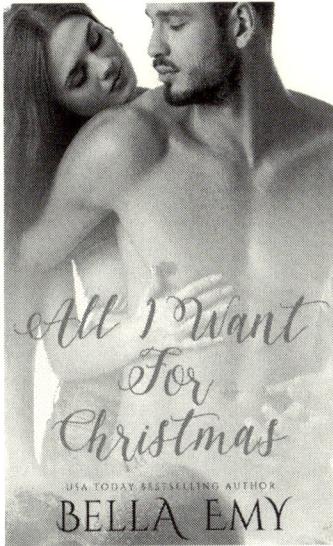

The All I Want Series

ALL I WANT FOR CHRISTMAS

Scarlett Raines

I left my hometown when I was fresh out of high school looking for more.

I was a country girl, but I'd gone off to New York City to pursue my dream in the television world.

What I didn't expect were my feelings for Cole Walker to come rushing back the instant I heard his name.

But who was I fooling?

I'd be going back home after the holidays, and the thought of being with him was just a fantasy of mine, like it had always been.

Cole Walker

When Scarlett-Mae Raines left Willowview, Texas, I thought I'd lost my chance with her forever.

She was now a city girl, and what would a cowboy like me have to offer her?

The day my eyes locked with hers once more after years of her being gone, I knew I had to find a way to make her mine.

I had one chance, one shot to give it my all, and this time, I wasn't going to let her walk away.

b e l l a   e m y
INTERNATIONAL BESTSELLING AUTHOR

a l l   i   w a n t
forever
THE ALL I WANT SERIES BOOK TWO

ALL I WANT FOREVER

Jenny-Rae Raines

All my life, I've been in and out of relationships hopping into the bed of one man right after the other.

No strings attached, no emotions involved.

When I finally did end up falling in love, I wound up with a broken heart.

I swore I'd never fall in love again.

One night, I said screw it all, and hooked up with Dustin Walker.

He's the total cowboy perfect for my country heart and soul.

Every time we get together, the connection is beyond compare.

He makes me feel like no one else does.

But I can't give into my temptation and continue sleeping with Dustin just because he owns my body like no one else ever has.

I need to keep my distance and just walk away before I fall in love again.

But every time I take a step forward, I end up taking two steps back and always wind up right back in his bed.

Dustin Walker

Once upon a time, I met a beautiful girl, fell in love, and swept her off her feet... or so I thought.

We were married, but not long after, I caught her rolling around in the sack with her ex.

Since the day we divorced, I promised myself I would never be in another relationship for as long as I lived.

I was content just sleeping around and not getting involved with anyone... until Jenny-Rae Raines wound up in my arms.

My eyes landed on her beautiful face and sexy little body, and I was done for.

Jenny is a naughty little vixen, and I just can't keep my thoughts, or hands, off of her.

But ever since the last time we slept together, Jenny has been keeping her distance from me.

I know she feels the chemistry we have toward one another just as badly as I do.

I just need to find a way to make her mine once and for all.

She's all I want forever, and I have no problem spending the rest of my life proving that to her if need be.

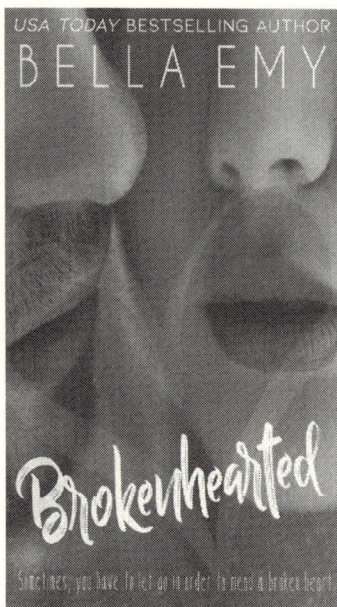

USA TODAY BESTSELLING AUTHOR

BELLA EMY

Brokenhearted

Sometimes, you have to let go in order to mend a broken heart

BROKENHEARTED

Could you love someone after learning the truth of his or her family's past?

Could you forgive someone after they've done the impossible?

Emily Jones has the perfect life.

She's married to a handsome man, has a career she loves, and amazing friends all around.

She's carefree and happy with the way everything has fallen into place for her–till one day it all comes crashing down on her. Her husband, Bruce, demands a divorce, and she is left utterly brokenhearted.

She's completely devastated and fears she cannot go on.

Then one day, a handsome stranger walks into her life–a stranger whom actually is more familiar to Emily than she realizes. Will she be able to let go of Bruce and start anew? Or will her broken heart hold her back from loving again?

Sometimes your first love isn't your one true love...

Sometimes you have to overcome what's holding you back in order to move forward...

Sometimes, you have to let go in order to mend a broken heart.

For more books, please visit

www.BellaEmy.com

Follow Bella

To stay up to date with all things Bella, you can follow Bella at any, or all, of these sites:

Facebook Page: bit.ly/BellaEmyFB
Book Group: bit.ly/BellaEmyFBGroup
Twitter: bit.ly/BellaEmyTwitter
Instagram: bit.ly/BellaEmyIG
Pinterest: bit.ly/BellaEmyPinterest
Goodreads: bit.ly/BellaEmyGR
Amazon: bit.ly/BellaEmyAmazon
Bookbub: bit.ly/BellaEmyBookbub
Order Paperbacks: bit.ly/BellasSignedPaperbacks
Website: www.bellaemy.com
Newsletter: bit.ly/BellaEmySubscribe

Bella Emy

USA Today Bestselling Author
Breaking hearts one story at a time

Made in the USA
Middletown, DE
29 September 2020